FROM THE
NANCY DREW FILES

THE CASE: Nancy investigates the murder of San Francisco supermodel Ursula Biemann.

CONTACT: Ned's cousin Laurel has just gotten married; her new husband, Evan, is an agent for Jane Zachary Associates . . . Ursula's former employer.

SUSPECTS: Sean McKearn—Ursula's ex-boyfriend's bitterness and jealousy over the breakup may have led him to a crime of passion.

Tina Grayce—Her ambition is to be San Francisco's top model, but Ursula always stood in the way . . . until now.

Marty Prince—He owns the rival Top Flight talent agency, and word is if you refuse to work for him, you don't work for anybody.

COMPLICATIONS: Ned is offered a role in a cola commercial, and his costar is the beautiful Amanda Syms. Nancy's trying to focus on the case but can't help wondering if she's lost Ned—and her heart—in San Francisco.

Books in The Nancy Drew Files® Series

Available from ARCHWAY Paperbacks

The Nancy-Drew Files™

Case 75

A Talent For Murder

Carolyn Keene

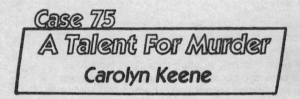

AN ARCHWAY PAPERBACK
Published by POCKET BOOKS
New York   London   Toronto   Sydney   Tokyo   Singapore

AN ARCHWAY PAPERBACK *Original*

An Archway Paperback published by
POCKET BOOKS, a division of Simon & Schuster Inc.
1230 Avenue of the Americas, New York, NY 10020

Copyright © 1992 by Simon & Schuster Inc.
Produced by Mega-Books of New York, Inc.

ISBN: 0-671-73079-7

First Archway Paperback printing September 1992

10 9 8 7 6 5 4 3 2

NANCY DREW, AN ARCHWAY PAPERBACK and colophon are registered trademarks of Simon & Schuster Inc.

THE NANCY DREW FILES is a trademark of Simon & Schuster Inc.

Cover art by Tricia Zimic

Printed in the U.S.A.

IL 6+

Chapter

One

CHECK OUT THAT GIRL. Haven't I seen her on TV?" Ned Nickerson whispered. He leaned close to Nancy Drew and gestured toward a willowy brunette in black leggings and a long, bulky red sweater.

The young woman had just entered the waiting room of Jane Zachary Associates, where Ned and Nancy were sitting on a soft leather couch. Waving to the receptionist, the brunette disappeared through an interior door.

Nancy nodded. "She's in those ads for Belle Cosmetics." The girl was pretty but not as stunning as she looked on TV with the help of professional makeup and lighting. "You recognized her awfully fast, Nickerson," Nancy said, nudging her boyfriend. "Got an eye for brunettes?"

THE NANCY DREW FILES

"Who, me?" Ned's brown eyes glimmered as he smiled. "I prefer a certain redhead with a talent for solving mysteries."

Nancy tucked a lock of reddish blond hair behind her ear as she gazed at Ned. She loved the way his smile lit up his handsome face. After a summer of fun, adventure—and romance—in Europe, Nancy had been glad to see Ned, her longtime boyfriend.

But her heart was still reeling from her summer romance with Mick Devlin, an Australian guy who shared her passion for mystery. Although she'd fallen for Mick, Nancy had realized that it wouldn't work out in the long run. Now she was back in the States, where she belonged.

The question is, do Ned and I belong together? Nancy thought. It was the main reason she had agreed to accompany Ned for a ten-day vacation in San Francisco. In a way, this trip could make or break their relationship.

The invitation from Ned's cousin, Laurel Franklin Chandler, had come at just the right time. Ned hadn't yet started his fall term at Emerson College, and who could resist a ten-day stay in a big, beautiful house overlooking San Francisco Bay?

Nancy and Ned had arrived the previous afternoon. The Chandlers' house, in the city's Marina District, was lovely. Ned and Nancy each had a spacious room with a view of the Golden Gate Bridge. It was shaping up to be a fantastic trip.

Laurel's husband, Evan, was an agent at Jane Zachary Associates, the city's top talent agency. JZA represented many of the area's hottest actors and models. When ad agencies needed actors or models for TV commercials or magazine ads, they came to JZA to flip through photos of their clientele. Often JZA clients landed high-paying assignments, which boosted their careers as well as the agency's reputation. Everytime a JZA client got the work, the agency got a commission.

Evan had been explaining the business to Nancy and Ned over dinner the night before when an idea had struck him. Evan had asked Nancy and Ned if they'd like to accompany him as a commercial was being filmed. Of course, the teens had jumped at the offer.

As they waited for Evan, who was taking care of business in his office, a steady stream of glamorous clients came and went through the double glass doors that led to the elevators. Watching the traffic, Ned shook his head. "Evan is one lucky guy. Can you imagine working around these beauties every day?"

"The guys are hunks, too," Nancy replied, though she had to admit that the parade of pretty women was making her feel a little plain. She glanced down at her black jeans and aqua blouse. The shirt set off her blue eyes nicely, but surrounded by models, she felt underdressed.

At last, the door to the offices opened, and Evan Chandler, a lanky man with curly brown hair, appeared. "Sorry to keep you waiting," he said.

Nancy looked up at Evan, whose energetic smile and friendly green eyes made her feel instantly welcome. He was followed by a blond woman in her late thirties. Dressed in a raw silk suit and suede heels, she was sleek and elegant.

"Jane," Evan said, "meet my wife's cousin, Ned Nickerson, and his girlfriend, Nancy Drew. This is Jane Zachary, my boss."

"Hi." Jane shook hands with Nancy and Ned, her gray eyes studying Ned intently. "Evan, your cousin is a knockout. Ever do any acting, Ned?"

Ned chuckled. "I once played a pilgrim in a fourth-grade Thanksgiving pageant." Nancy and Evan laughed, but Jane remained serious.

"No, really," she insisted, "you've got the right stuff. You could do well in this business."

"But I don't act," Ned protested.

Jane made a gesture of dismissal. "With your looks, who cares? Commercials don't need great acting. I'll bet the camera would like you, though we'd have to test you to be sure."

Ned caught Nancy's eye and grinned in disbelief. "Thanks for the compliment," he said. "But this is just a vacation. I'm in the process of earning a degree at Emerson College."

"Finish your education, by all means," Jane replied. "But after you graduate—"

"Evan!" A stout young man emerged from the

doorway to the JZA offices. "Nob Hill Studios is on the phone, and they say it's urgent. Line two."

"Thanks, Ziggy," Evan said, walking to the receptionist's desk. "That's where we're going to watch the shoot," he explained to Nancy and Ned as he picked up the phone.

"Evan Chandler here. Hi, Sid . . . She's not? When was she due? . . . Really?" He looked at his watch and frowned. Nancy saw Jane approach Evan, a look of concern on her face.

Evan continued. "Did you call her apartment? . . . No, she's always been dependable. . . . Okay, I'm on my way. I'll put someone on it from this end. Right." He hung up, scowling.

"What's the problem?" Jane demanded.

Evan shook his head. "Ursula Biemann hasn't shown up for the shoot. She was due by eight-thirty this morning, which makes her almost two hours late."

"She's an actress?" Nancy asked.

Evan nodded, looking distracted. "One of the busiest." He pointed to one of the photographs arranged on a wall. "That's her." Ursula was a striking young woman with round, soulful eyes, high cheekbones, and a wide, expressive mouth. "She's in that commercial we're shooting today."

Jane had begun to pace nervously in front of the reception desk. "Ursula's *never* late," she said. "Evan, you'd better get over to the studio, before they go crazy." Nancy noted that Jane was gnawing on her lower lip, her look of cool elegance giving way to worry.

"Ziggy!" Evan called. The squat young man who had called Evan to the phone reappeared. "Ziggy Matson, my assistant," he said, introducing Nancy and Ned to the man with stubby blond hair and a fleshy face.

"Ursula Biemann is a no-show," Evan said.

Ziggy pursed his lips in a soundless whistle. "What should I do?" he asked.

"Keep calling her place," said the agent. "Leave word with her service for her to contact us immediately. Start calling actresses on our list and see who's available. The producers might want to replace her. You'll be able to reach me at the studio or on my car phone." Nancy was impressed by Evan's poise and decisiveness.

"Right," Ziggy said, ducking behind the door to the offices.

"I'm out of here," Evan told Jane. "Coming?" he asked Nancy and Ned.

"You're sure we won't be in the way?" Ned asked.

"Trust me, no one will notice you in the chaos," Evan said as he led the way through the doors and down the elevator. In the underground garage of the glass and steel office building, Nancy gave Evan's sleek sports car an admiring glance.

"Cross your fingers," Evan said as they fastened their seat belts. "If we're lucky, Ursula will be there when we arrive."

A ten-minute drive took them to Nob Hill Studios, a three-story building in an industrial district. Nancy and Ned followed Evan through a lobby hung with framed movie posters. After speaking with a receptionist, he pushed open a steel door labeled Stage 1, and Nancy found herself in a huge room that resembled a dark, empty warehouse.

Dozens of people were clustered in one corner, where a modern kitchen was surrounded by cameras and lights. The crew talked in hushed voices. Some sat glumly in canvas director's chairs, sipping from paper cups, while others paced nervously.

"Evan!" The shout came from a harried-looking, balding man in his forties, who ran to meet them. He was casually dressed in khaki pants and a denim shirt, though his hand-tooled leather boots were obviously expensive.

"You find her yet?" he demanded.

Evan shook his head. "No such luck."

The man glanced at his watch and groaned. "This is costing a fortune." He waved at the milling workers, adding, "I'm paying them to wait around, and the equipment rental is—"

"Can you work around her?" Evan asked.

"Work *around* her?" The man looked ready to cry. "She's in every shot! We're stuck!"

Evan put a hand on the agitated man's shoulder. "Take it easy, Sid. I'll call and see if Ursula's been located. If she's still missing, you and the account executives can probably arrange for a replacement within the hour. You'll be able to start up after lunch."

Sid nodded and made an effort to calm down. He was about to turn back to the crew when he noticed Ned and Nancy standing behind Evan.

"This is Ned Nickerson and Nancy Drew," said Evan. "They're in town on vacation. Guys, meet Sid Pearl, the producer of this commercial."

"If there *is* a commercial," Sid muttered.

"I need a phone," Evan called to a passing assistant, who hustled off. He turned to Ned and Nancy. "If you'll excuse me . . ."

"No problem," Ned told him.

"Why don't we take a walk, and get out of the way?" Nancy suggested. "We'll be back," she assured Evan, who waved.

Outside, the fog that had covered the city earlier had vanished. The sky was clear and blue, the sunshine dazzling.

Ned looked up and down the street, which was lined on both sides with drab industrial buildings. "Hmm," Ned said thoughtfully. "It's not exactly a tourist's dream around here, is it?"

Nancy pointed to the end of the block where a green awning marked Café shaded the sidewalk.

"That looks like our only choice. Let's head over and get something cold to drink."

"Okay," Ned said, adding, "Poor Sid. I wonder what's keeping Ursula?"

"I'm sure everyone on the crew is wondering the same thing," Nancy said as they walked away from the studio entrance. The stucco facade of the building stretched ahead, ending at an alley.

Ned laughed. "Can you believe Jane Zachary thinking I could make it as an actor? I mean, can you picture me in— Nancy? What's wrong?"

Nancy had stopped short and was staring intently down the alley. In the shadowed recess was a large, square object, and lying in front of it was a woman's shoe. Something about the shoe triggered a feeling of alarm inside Nancy.

"What is it?" Ned repeated.

"Probably nothing," Nancy replied, slowly making her way into the alley. "Just curious."

Picking up the elegant shoe, she saw that it was an imported brand made of soft blue leather— definitely out of place in this grimy passageway.

The large object turned out to be a shipping carton, which almost filled the width of the alley. She squeezed by it, feeling a sudden chill of anticipation.

"Ned!" she gasped. Her heart twisted at the sight of a motionless body. A young woman lay sprawled behind the carton.

"What is it?" Ned asked, pushing past the

carton. When he took in the grim scene, his face paled with shock.

Nancy bent down to study the girl's face. A large, discolored bruise was visible on her temple. Still, somehow the woman's lovely features seemed familiar. Where had Nancy seen those high cheekbones and the wide, expressive mouth?

Suddenly her mind flashed back to the huge glossy posters in the JZA reception area. There was no mistaking this face. She slowly straightened up. Her throat felt tight and constricted.

"We'd better get Evan," she said quietly. "I think we've just found Ursula Biemann."

Chapter

Two

NANCY KNELT to confirm what she feared—
there was no pulse, no breath, no sign of life.

Ned stood stock-still, eyes fixed on the corpse.
"Is she—"

Nancy nodded. "I'm afraid so. Go get Evan,
but don't tell anyone else. I'll wait here."

As Ned raced away, Nancy stood up, fighting
hard to ignore the shaky feeling in the pit of her
stomach. It wasn't the first time she'd seen a dead
body, but the sight was always upsetting. Taking
care not to disturb possible evidence, she
checked out the alley.

A jagged hunk of concrete sat a few feet from
the body. Could it have been the weapon used on
Ursula? Nancy saw no sign of blood but decided
to point out the concrete to the police.

She studied the body. The dead girl was dressed in a violet silk, off-the-shoulder evening dress. She wore a slender gold necklace and a slim watch with a gold band.

One foot was bare. The other leg was awkwardly folded. Nancy saw that the sole of the shoe was almost unworn, but there was an ugly scuff mark on the back of the heel. She found the other shoe similarly disfigured.

Near the body was a fancy, beaded purse. With a pencil from her own purse, Nancy gently lifted the flap and peered in. She saw a wallet and a business card stashed beside it. Squinting, Nancy could make out the print on the card: Top Flight Artists, Marty Prince.

Nancy turned to the cardboard carton that had concealed the body. On it was a shipping label with an address on the same block as the studio.

"Nancy!" Ned ran down the alley with Evan following behind him. As the agent pushed past the carton and saw Ursula, he groaned.

"That's her," Evan said faintly. He sagged against the wall and closed his eyes. "This is awful, horrible. . . . What do we do now?"

"First you call the police," Nancy answered.

Evan nodded. His face was chalky white.

"Then see that everyone stays put until the police say otherwise." Nancy looked closely at Evan. "Are you all right?"

Evan took a shaky breath. "I guess so," he said. "My wife told me about your detective work. I

12

guess you've seen this kind of thing, but I'm not used to it. What happened to her?"

"That's not for me to say," Nancy said. "Ned and I will wait for you out here."

While Evan went back inside, Ned and Nancy walked out to the street. Nancy's detective instincts were stirring, and at the same time her hopes for a quiet, romantic vacation were fading.

"What do you make of it?" Ned asked.

"From the bruise on her temple, I'd guess that someone hit her," Nancy said. "Though she could have fallen and bumped her head on something. It doesn't look like robbery, since she's still wearing gold jewelry and her purse seems to be—"

"The police are on the way," Evan called, striding up the alley. "Sid's handling things inside."

Sirens wailed in the distance. A few minutes later, police cars pulled up at the curb. Uniformed officers scrambled out, and a tall, thin man in a brown suit got out of an unmarked car. He walked up, fastening a gold badge to the breast pocket of his jacket.

"Lieutenant Antonio, San Francisco Police Department, Homicide," he said. His wide, thin-lipped mouth and jutting jaw seemed to be set in a permanent scowl as he eyed Nancy, Ned, and Evan. "Who found the body?"

"I did," Nancy replied, facing the tall man. "It's down that alley, hidden by a big carton."

"Wait here," said the lieutenant. He walked down the alley, followed by officers carrying a camera and large cases.

By the time the lieutenant returned, two officers were blocking off the area with crime-scene tape. Antonio summoned another officer and approached Nancy, Ned, and Evan.

"Let's get some statements," he said.

As the other officer took out a pad and pencil, Sid rushed up to the group.

"I called Jane. She's on her way. What—" He stopped as Lieutenant Antonio glared at him.

"Who are you?" demanded the gruff lieutenant.

"I'm Sid Pearl, the producer—"

"Wait inside with the others, Mr. Pearl. I'll get to you shortly." He faced Nancy. "Let's hear how it happened."

Nancy told him about finding the body. "I noticed a piece of concrete nearby," she added. "It might be important."

"My officers are very observant," the lieutenant said dryly. "I'm sure they'll see the concrete, too. Mr. Nickerson?"

Ned confirmed Nancy's story, and the uniformed officer took it all down in shorthand.

When Ned had finished, Antonio swung his gaze to Evan. "You identified the body, Mr. Chandler?"

Evan nodded. "That's right. I—"

"What was your connection with the deceased?" the lieutenant asked crisply.

"I'm a talent agent—she's—" Evan stammered, clearly shaken. "Ursula *was* a client, an actress and model. She was due to work here today, and Sid called me at the agency when she didn't show."

"Are these two with the agency, too?" the lieutenant asked, indicating Nancy and Ned.

"Ned is my wife's cousin," Evan explained. "He and Nancy are visiting San Francisco."

"Tourists," the lieutenant grumbled, then continued his questions. "Did Ms. Biemann have a habit of missing appointments?"

"No," Evan insisted. "Ursula was reliable and businesslike, at least until recently."

"What happened recently?" Nancy asked.

"For one thing, she just broke up with her boyfriend, Sean—" Evan began, but Lieutenant Antonio stopped him with an upraised hand.

"Just a minute," he snapped. "It's not your place to ask questions, Ms. Drew, just to answer them. Is that clear?"

"Sorry," Nancy said. "Force of habit."

The lieutenant narrowed his eyes at her. "What is that supposed to mean?"

"Nancy's had some experience with detective work," Ned explained.

A sarcastic smile appeared on Lieutenant Antonio's face. "Is that a fact? Do you have a license?"

"I'm not a professional," Nancy said, bristling at the older man's dismissive attitude.

The lieutenant frowned. "Let's get one thing straight," he said. "I don't have much use for private investigators, and none at all for amateurs. If I find you've meddled in police business, you'll be very sorry. Understood?"

"There's no call for threats," Ned protested.

The lieutenant ignored him. "Understood?" he repeated softly.

"Absolutely," Nancy replied. She realized it would be foolish to get on this man's bad side, and she always tried to cooperate with the police.

Antonio's stare moved from Nancy to Ned. "Did either of you see the deceased before today?"

"We live two thousand miles away, and we never saw Ursula Biemann until we found her body," Ned said.

"How long have you been in San Francisco?" the lieutenant pressed.

When Nancy explained that they'd arrived the previous afternoon, Antonio frowned and asked, "Do you have witnesses who will vouch for your whereabouts last night?"

Nancy had just answered the question when a large car pulled to the curb, and she saw Jane Zachary jump out, along with a short, wiry man with slicked-back hair. They immediately rushed over to join the group.

"I got here as soon as I could," Jane said, crossing to Evan's side. "This is a tragedy."

Before the lieutenant could respond to the woman's arrival, a new voice rang out, "There he is! That's the one!"

The outburst came from the man who had arrived with Jane. Nancy had never seen him in her life, but now he had stepped forward, his eyes wide, and his index finger rigidly extended.

He was pointing straight at Ned!

Chapter

Three

Nancy was astonished. What was this man talking about?

The lieutenant looked at the stranger with suspicion. "There *who* is?" he asked.

"The one we want!" The wiry man circled the mystified Ned, studying his face from various angles. "He's *perfect.*" He clapped his hands and spun around to Jane. "Where were you hiding him?"

Jane sighed. "He's not an actor, Freddy." She looked at the lieutenant. "Sorry. I'm Jane Zachary of Jane Zachary Associates. This is Freddy Estevez of Burton-Freeley Advertising, in charge of the King Kola account. We were auditioning actors for a commercial when we heard about Ursula."

"We've got our man!" Freddy exclaimed. "Tall, athletic, great eyes—"

"Wait a minute," Ned protested.

"Quiet!" the lieutenant roared. "I hate to bother you with trivia like a police investigation, but can I assume you're not accusing Mr. Nickerson of any criminal acts?"

"Of course not," Freddy said, shrinking away from the angry lieutenant.

Antonio let out a breath and gave Ned and Nancy a hard look. "Then that's all for now, but don't leave town without clearing it with me." He turned to Jane. "I'll want to talk to you later."

"I'll be at my office," she answered, handing him a business card.

After telling one officer to notify Ursula's family of the death, Antonio told the other officers, "Let's get statements from the people inside."

As Nancy watched the police file into the studio, Jane put an arm around Evan's shoulders. "Poor Ursula. I can't believe it! And how terrible for you, having to identify her body." Her carefully penciled eyebrows knitted in a frown. "Could her death have anything to do with Marty—"

"Not now, Jane!" Evan exclaimed quickly, looking around. "We'll talk back at JZA. And I'd like Nancy and Ned to sit in."

Walking to Evan's car, Ned took Nancy's

hand. From the confused look in his eyes, she could see that Ned was trying to sort out the strange events.

"What a crazy day," he said. "Do you think Evan wants you to investigate?"

Nancy wondered the same thing. She was torn between her wish for a vacation with Ned and the strong curiosity that always kicked in when she stumbled on a mystery like Ursula's death. She wanted to know about the ex-boyfriend Evan had talked about, as well as the man named Marty, whom Jane had mentioned. Was it the Marty Prince whose card had been in Ursula's purse?

"I guess we'll find out if Evan wants me to investigate when we get back to the agency," Nancy said. The real question in her mind was: How would she respond if she was asked?

During the ride back, Nancy turned to Evan. "What did you mean about Ursula not being her usual self lately?"

"She broke up with this guy Sean McKearn a month ago," Evan explained. "McKearn has a nasty temper and didn't want to let her go. He'd been pestering her night and day ever since, making her crazy. . . . There was something else."

Evan broke off, looking troubled. "Should we be talking about this? The lieutenant said not to get involved."

"I'm not involved," Nancy pointed out. "Just

curious. Jane mentioned the name Marty. Did she mean Marty Prince, of Top Flight Artists?"

Evan nodded. "Exactly. Top Flight is a new agency in town, and Marty Prince is the guy who runs it. How do you know about him?"

Nancy told him about the card in Ursula's purse. "Tell me about him," she urged.

"Marty wants Top Flight to be competitive with JZA, and he wants it *now,*" Evan explained. "He figures the quickest way to success is to get our best talent to leave us and sign with him."

"Is that legal?" Ned asked.

"Our usual talent contracts run for a year," Evan explained. "When the contract runs out, the talent can sign with anyone he or she wants. So an agent could call an actor and say, 'Go with me and I'll get you more auditions, more work, negotiate for better money.' That's fair. But we heard a rumor that Marty is using tactics that may be illegal."

"Such as?" Nancy prompted.

"No one will talk openly about it," Evan admitted, "but apparently pressure is being put on talent to switch, even if they're happy with us."

"How?" Nancy asked, growing more interested.

"Actors and models are in a competitive field," Evan said. "A rumor that so-and-so is always late, can't learn dialogue, or is on an ego trip can ruin a career. The threat of it can be scary."

21

As Evan reached his parking spot in the building's garage, he added, "And there's an even worse threat—violence. People who rely on their looks are terrified of being scarred for life."

"You think Ursula was threatened?" Ned asked.

As they got into the elevator, the agent replied, "Another actress told my assistant, Ziggy, that Ursula had gotten anonymous notes saying that if she didn't go to Top Flight, she wouldn't stay as pretty as she was."

"Hmm," Nancy mused. "An ex-boyfriend with a temper, and a greedy agent who's up to dirty tricks." It had the makings of a fascinating case.

Nancy was mulling over suspects when they entered the JZA reception area and found Freddy Estevez, the advertising man, chatting with the receptionist.

"I've been waiting for you—with an offer you can't refuse," Freddy said, clapping Ned on the back. "This King Kola ad will get lots of network play. That means big bucks for the actors. Plus, it'll be fun."

"But I'm not an actor," Ned insisted.

"Hey, it's not Shakespeare," Freddy replied. "We just show this cute young couple having fun while they drink King Kola. One sequence will be riding in a hot-air balloon in Napa Valley."

"Really?" Ned asked, his interest piqued. "A hot-air balloon?"

"Hey, let's get you on videotape," Freddy said. "Who knows, maybe you won't look as good on screen as you do in the flesh."

Ned looked at Nancy, who shrugged. "It can't hurt to try, I guess," he said.

"Great!" Freddy exclaimed, whisking Ned through the door to the offices. Nancy and Evan followed them into a large room that had work stations sectioned off by smoked glass screens. The room buzzed with conversation and ringing phones. A glass wall on Nancy's right revealed a large conference room. The wall to her left contained doors to window offices.

"Amanda!" Freddy called. "Where are you?"

A girl with stylishly short cinnamon-colored hair emerged from one work station. She was just about Nancy's height, with a dynamite figure. "Here I am," she said, approaching Ned with a directness that set Nancy off-balance.

"This is Amanda Syms, the model you'd be working with," Freddy said to Ned. "Let's get you two on video, so we can see if there's chemistry between you."

"I can feel chemistry already," Amanda said, her green eyes sparkling as she looked up at Ned.

Nancy felt a blush heat her face as she watched her boyfriend grin at the model. Here she was, stung by jealousy, while Ned seemed to be having the time of his life. Be happy for him, Nancy told herself. This could be his big break.

But as they followed Freddy down a corridor,

Nancy couldn't shake off the feeling that Ned's "show biz break" was going to put a crimp in their romance.

Freddy ushered the star couple into an office. Through the open door Nancy could see Ziggy behind a video camera. Nancy was about to step inside when Freddy blocked her path.

"Would you mind waiting outside?" he asked. "It's kind of crowded in here. We won't be long."

Feeling awkward, Nancy went back to the main room and found her way to Evan's office.

"Sit down," he said as Nancy entered the sleek office furnished with chrome tables and black leather chairs. "You can wait here while they film Wonder Boy," he teased. "Maybe Jane is right about Ned. He could become a hot property."

"You never know," she said, forcing a smile. Unpleasant images paraded through Nancy's mind: Ned surrounded by gorgeous girls, becoming a celebrity, losing interest in her.

Evan excused himself to make a call, and Nancy leafed through a magazine, unable to concentrate.

After what seemed like a long time, she heard Ned's voice—accompanied by the ring of female laughter. Nancy joined them in the main room.

"He looks even better on screen!" Freddy crowed. "Real star quality! The only problem is the name."

"The name?" Ned echoed.

"In commercials, it doesn't matter, but in TV and movies you need a name that's more now, more hot, like . . . Derek. Derek Nichols!"

"I like Derek," Amanda said. "It's cute."

"Slow down." Ned laughed. "I think I'll stick with plain old Ned. I'm used to it." He looked over at Nancy. "Right, Nan?"

Nancy smiled up at him. "I've always loved it myself."

"So, what do you say, Ned?" Freddy asked. "If you want the job, it's yours."

"Well . . ." Ned glanced back at Nancy, who gave him what she hoped looked like an encouraging smile. "As long as we'll still have plenty of time together here, I'll do it. I'd love to!"

Nancy turned away to hide her disappointment. She knew that Ned would have passed up the offer if he knew how she really felt, but she wasn't about to stand in his way.

"Great!" Freddy exclaimed. "I'll set up a wardrobe fitting for you tomorrow." Just then Jane came out of her office, and Freddy called out, "Ned's going to do it! I'll arrange the wardrobe appointment. Come along, Amanda, and we'll work out your schedule for tomorrow." He bustled off to one of the work stations.

Amanda gave Ned another dazzling smile that was like a knife through Nancy's heart. "Don't be nervous," Amanda told Ned. "We're going to hit it off just fine." Then she followed Freddy.

25

"This is good news." Jane smiled warmly at Ned. "We'll call you at Evan's house to let you know when—"

"Is it true?" cried a shrill voice from the corridor.

Nancy turned and saw a tall young woman with flaming red hair and a rail-thin figure. Tears sparkled in her bright blue eyes.

The young woman strode up to Jane, her delicate face pale with tension. "I just heard Freddy—is Ursula really dead?"

"Yes, Tina, I'm afraid so," Jane said quietly. "Her body was found this morning. Her family has been notified, and the police are trying to determine how she died."

"I already know how she died." Although Tina's voice shook, every word she said was crystal clear. "Ursula was murdered. And I know who is responsible!"

Chapter

Four

NANCY STUDIED TINA, who was visibly shaking. Her hands were clenched into white-knuckled fists, and her eyes darted around as though looking for unseen dangers. The room had gone silent at Tina's shrill announcement.

Gently, Jane patted her shoulder. "Tina, take it easy." She pulled out a desk chair from one of the work stations, and Tina sat down. Her breathing was shallow, and Nancy thought she might faint.

Jane turned to her assistant, who had risen from her desk and was regarding Tina with concern. "Holly," Jane ordered, "get Tina some water." The young woman nodded and walked quickly down the corridor.

Jane bent to speak to Tina quietly. "Tina, dear, why don't we talk in my office. It'll be more private, all right?"

"All right," Tina muttered weakly.

Evan stuck his head out of his office. "Is something wrong? I heard—" He noticed the distraught, pale actress. "Tina?"

"She has information about Ursula's death," Jane said. "We'll discuss it in my office."

"Maybe Nancy and Ned should join us," Evan said. "Nancy might be willing to help us out."

"Would you?" Jane asked, looking tired and tense. "I've been worried sick lately. There's been so much going on, and now this horrible news about Ursula—"

She paused when Holly returned with a cup of water, which she handed to Tina. The girl took a drink and relaxed a little.

"Come on," Jane said, helping Tina to her office. "Holly, no calls or interruptions."

Situated at the head of the corridor, Jane's office was large and sunny. One whole wall was glass, with a panoramic view of the bay. A huge desk was covered with photographs and scripts. Fine antique chairs surrounded a coffee table, which was polished to a gleaming finish. Nancy's eyes were drawn to a stunning hanging Oriental rug.

Once everyone was seated, Evan introduced Nancy and Ned to Tina Grayce, another JZA client.

"Were you and Ursula close?" Nancy asked gently.

Tina nodded. "We'd gotten close lately. We

saw each other at auditions a lot, and sometimes we went out to lunch. Ursula liked talking to me, and lately she'd needed someone to talk to."

"What about?" Nancy asked.

Tina swallowed the rest of the water, then fiddled with the cup. "Her troubles. Ursula's ex-boyfriend was giving her a hard time."

Jane frowned. "Sean McKearn is a disturbed young man. Ursula brought him to our Christmas party last year, and they had a terrible fight. Sean got into a jealous rage when Ursula said hello to a male model. I was afraid Sean was going to attack Nelson, so I had security remove Sean from the party. Ursula was very upset."

"Is Sean an actor, too?" Ned asked.

"Are you kidding?" Tina said scornfully. "He says it's for wimps."

"He's a sculptor and woodworker," Jane said. "He's good-looking enough, but he doesn't exactly have a winning personality."

"That's putting it mildly," Tina agreed. "He's going to get into real trouble one day. He already has a police record for assault."

"Really?" Nancy leaned forward. "Do you know any details about that?"

Tina blinked, then said, "No, it's just something Ursula mentioned."

"Do you think he might have assaulted Ursula?" Ned asked.

Nodding vigorously, Tina said, "Absolutely. If he got mad enough, he'd do it."

Nancy made a mental note about Sean. "I'd like to talk to this Nelson some time soon."

"I'm sure he'd like to talk to you, too," Evan said grinning. "He likes attractive girls."

Tina dropped the paper cup on the table. "Ursula was getting threats, too. Ugly ones. Unsigned notes and phone calls in the middle of the night."

"Do you think Sean was behind the threatening notes and calls?" Ned asked.

Tina folded her arms across her chest. "No. He'd rant and rave—but threatening notes? That's not Sean's style." She hesitated. "Before I go on, you have to promise not to tell anyone, okay? I don't want to end up like Ursula."

"We won't say a word," Jane assured her.

"Well—" Tina hesitated, taking a deep breath. "I think it's Marty Prince. He wanted Ursula to sign with Top Flight, the new agency, and she wouldn't do it."

"I *knew* it!" Jane cried, slamming her hand on her desktop. "I knew it was Marty!"

Recalling the card in Ursula's purse, Nancy said, "Tina, did Ursula actually say that the threats came from Marty Prince?"

"Ursula said that the threats started *after* she told Marty she was staying with JZA. At first he just warned her that she'd regret her decision. Then he tried to meet with her, but she refused. That's when the really nasty stuff began."

"What kind of stuff?" Nancy asked.

"Someone sent Ursula a photo of herself from a magazine ad. But they'd penciled in cuts and scars and written, 'This could be you.'" Tina shuddered. "Then some guy called, hinting that acid could ruin a girl's face and end a career."

"Why didn't she tell us?" Jane asked. "She must have been going out of her mind."

"She was too scared to talk," Tina answered. "She only told me in desperation. She said she'd go crazy if she didn't tell someone."

Ned whistled. "This Marty Prince sounds like bad news. How does he get away with it?"

Evan scowled. "He's clever. We can't prove anything. When he started Top Flight, he bought ads and sent out mailings to attract clients. That got him some talent, but not top money-makers. So he went after people like Ursula, who were always working."

"Tina, who else was threatened?" Jane asked.

"They're too frightened to say," Tina said.

"What about you?" Nancy wanted to know.

"Me?" Tina gave Nancy a sad smile. "I don't rate that attention. I don't work that much."

"Tina," Evan said, looking at her earnestly, "you need to report this to the police."

"The police?" Tina stiffened. "I couldn't! What if Marty found out? If he knew Ursula talked to me, he might . . . no, I can't."

"They'll keep your name out of it," Ned assured her. "You want the people responsible for Ursula's death to be caught, don't you?"

Tina nodded. "Of course, but—"

"If you don't tell them, you could be in trouble," Nancy said. "You'd be withholding evidence of a crime. That's a crime, too."

Tina bit her lip, looking terrified. "I don't know what to do," she protested.

"The sooner the police get this information, the better," Nancy urged. "Why don't we call them and ask to speak to Lieutenant Antonio?"

"No!" Tina insisted, standing abruptly. "I mean . . . I'll tell the police, but give me time to calm down first. I'll call later, I promise."

"Just don't put it off," Nancy warned the frightened girl. "This information could be the key that helps the police find Ursula's killer."

Tina nodded, backing toward the door. "I'll call that lieutenant, what's his name?"

"Antonio," Nancy said.

"Right. As soon as I get home," she said. "Thanks for your help." Tina wiped the tears from her eyes, then slipped out of Jane's office.

Just then, Holly appeared in the doorway. "Excuse me, Jane. I know you wanted me to hold your calls, but there's a Lieutenant Antonio on the line. He wants to meet with you and Evan."

"Tell him we'll be here all day," Jane replied. Her eyes were dark with worry as she turned to Nancy. "Thanks for talking to Tina."

"Were Tina and Ursula close?" Nancy asked.

"I've seen them together a few times, having

lunch in a coffee shop near here," Evan said. "I guess they were pretty tight lately."

"If you don't mind my asking," Nancy said, "has Marty Prince hurt your business badly?"

Jane sighed and leaned back in her desk chair. "Marty has taken some valuable talent, and income is down. I've laid off two employees, and we're still struggling. Yes, he's hurt us. And I think he'd do anything to stop Ursula from signing up with us again—which she would have done if she hadn't been killed."

Evan drummed his fingers on the table. "If we can expose Marty's illegal activities, we'll stop the drain of talent and turn things around."

"Maybe I could help," Nancy said.

"I hate to ask when you're on vacation," Evan said, "but Laurel says you're good."

"So I'd be looking for proof that Marty Prince is engaging in criminal activities to pressure people to sign with his agency," Nancy said. "We don't know if he was involved in Ursula's death."

"I'd be surprised if he wasn't," Evan said.

Ned reached over and squeezed Nancy's hand. "I guess it's going to be a working vacation for both of us."

Nancy was surprised at Ned's willingness to go along with the case. As she stared into his warm brown eyes, an idea struck her. "Why don't you work as my undercover source? If you sign with

33

JZA, you'll be an insider. You might be able to find out who's getting pressured."

"Good idea!" Evan exclaimed.

"I'm game," Ned said, "if you think I can help."

"Definitely," Nancy said, squeezing his hand.

Jane nodded happily in agreement. "Come in tomorrow and I'll have papers for you to sign. We'll also set up a session for your head shots."

"Head shots?" Ned asked.

"Photos to show casting directors," Evan explained. "It's standard procedure. We'll send you to Mario, a photographer who shoots a lot of our people. He might be a good source of information, come to think of it."

"A wardrobe fitting, contracts to sign, and a photo session," Ned said, ticking them off on his fingers. "It's going to be a busy day."

Nancy smiled at Ned. If they couldn't spend the week relaxing together, at least they'd be working together. Maybe this vacation would stir up the excitement their romance needed.

Evan checked his watch. "If you two want to take off, you can use my car. Jane can drop me off later."

"Fine," Ned replied as he and Nancy rose. "It's probably just as well if we miss Antonio. We didn't exactly score points with him."

Nancy and Ned had just reached the reception area when Freddy Estevez called, "Ned! Got a minute?"

Turning, Nancy saw Freddy and Amanda peering out of the door to the offices. "The fitting is at eleven tomorrow," Freddy said. "Be here at ten-thirty, and I'll drive you over."

"No problem," Ned told him. "I have to come in tomorrow to sign a contract with JZA, anyway."

Amanda hooked an arm through Ned's. "You're signing here?" she asked. "Terrific. That means we'll be seeing a lot of each other from now on."

Nancy wasn't surprised by the melting look Amanda gave Ned. What *really* bothered her was the glowing smile that lit Ned's face.

Chapter

Five

"AREN'T THERE ANY BRAKES on this roller coaster?" Nancy asked as the car swooped around a dizzying curve.

"Sorry," Ned said, hitting the brakes. "I'm not used to driving on such steep streets."

As they drove back to the Chandlers' house Ned kept his eyes on the road. The streets of San Francisco snaked up pitched hills and down steep slopes lined with Victorian houses and tiny gardens.

"Tomorrow I'll get the word on Top Flight," Ned said as he turned onto the Chandlers' street. "The photographer might have heard rumors. And I can talk to Amanda."

"I'm sure *she'd* be happy to talk to you about anything," Nancy said, then regretted the comment the minute it slipped out.

Ned looked at her out of the corner of his eye as he pulled into the Chandlers' driveway. "What was that all about?" he asked, pulling to a stop. "Don't tell me you're jealous of Amanda?"

"That's not it," Nancy said, hesitating. "It would be silly to get jealous just because a beautiful girl starts batting her eyelashes at you." And you smile right back, she thought.

"It was your idea for me to go undercover at JZA," Ned said. "There are lots of pretty girls I'll have to talk to—in the line of duty. Are you going to get upset each time?"

Nancy felt foolish. "Of course not. I'm sorry for making a fuss about it."

"How do you think I feel when you're surrounded by great-looking guys?" Ned asked as he unbuckled his seat belt and turned to her. "It happens all the time when you're working on a case. But I trust you to handle them. I can handle Amanda."

"I know you can," Nancy said. Her worries faded as Ned reached over and wrapped his arms around her. She felt a little silly for being jealous, but at the same time she wasn't sure where she stood with Ned. Only time would tell.

"Would you buy something from a guy in this tie?" Ned asked as Nancy sat down at the breakfast table. He wore a navy blazer and a silk tie with diagonal stripes of red and black.

"I'd buy anything from you," Nancy said, pouring a glass of juice. "But I'm prejudiced."

The evening before, the Chandlers had taken Nancy and Ned across the Golden Gate Bridge for dinner in a restaurant tucked in a grove of huge redwoods. The delicious food and spectacular view had made for a magical evening.

"Is that all you're eating?" Laurel asked as Nancy took a spoonful of scrambled eggs and a slice of toast.

A petite woman with delicate features, Laurel Franklin Chandler wore her black hair in a short, pixie cut. Nancy had immediately hit it off with Ned's cousin, who looked eighteen, though she was twenty-four.

"After that gourmet dinner last night, I could swear off food for a week," Nancy assured her. "Besides, we have to get going soon."

"That's right," Ned agreed. "It's the first day of my new career, and I'd better be on time."

Evan had left for work, so Nancy and Ned would use the car they'd rented at the airport.

"Nancy, I'm so glad you're going to check out Marty Prince," Laurel said. "Poor Evan has been losing a lot of sleep over the problems at the agency."

"I hope we can help," Nancy said, draining her glass.

Ned stood up and put his breakfast plate in the sink. "Ready when you are, Ms. Detective."

It was a typical San Francisco morning, cool

and cloudy. As they passed Golden Gate Park, Ned glanced over at Nancy from behind the wheel.

"What are your plans today?" he asked.

Nancy had been considering her next steps. "I'd like to check out Ursula's apartment—if it hasn't already been sealed off by the police."

"Can you do that without getting in Lieutenant Antonio's way?" Ned asked.

"I'll do my best," Nancy said. "Then there's Top Flight Artists. I want to get a handle on Marty Prince. I'll need a plausible cover story before I approach him, though. I don't want Marty to know I'm checking him out."

Ned nodded. "Makes sense. And I'll nose around for any inside information."

At JZA they were whisked into Jane's office, where a stack of forms awaited Ned's signature.

"I thought I'd be signing just one contract," he said, staring at the pile of papers.

Jane laughed. "There are different contracts for each kind of work: commercials, film, TV, and so on. And three copies of each."

Ned was working his way to the bottom of the pile when Freddy Estevez popped in. His dark hair was slicked back and his expression was exuberant. He studied Ned's outfit and grinned. "Looking good."

After Ned signed the last contract, Jane stood up and shook his hand. "Welcome to our JZA family," she said brightly.

"You've signed?" Freddy asked. "Terrific. Listen, Amanda's here. I'll drive you to the fitting in just a minute, okay?"

"Sure," Ned replied. "I'll be outside."

Back in the reception area, Nancy and Ned found Amanda. She was wearing a dazzling gold lamé jumpsuit and a smile to match. "How's my new partner?" she asked, strolling over to Ned.

"Uh, fine," Ned said. He touched his collar as if it were uncomfortably tight. "Amanda, did you meet my girlfriend, Nancy Drew, yesterday?"

"Yeah—hi." Amanda gave Nancy a brief look before turning her attention back to Ned.

"You heard about Ursula Biemann?" Ned asked, lowering his voice. "The model who—"

Amanda's smile faded. "Wasn't it awful? I knew Ursula. I mean, we weren't friends, but we saw each other around." She leaned close to Ned and spoke in a hushed voice. "I'll bet that weird boyfriend did it. He's kind of scary."

"Oh?" Ned asked. "I heard talk about someone from a rival talent agency threatening her. Is it possible? Does this business get that rough?"

Ned caught Nancy's eye, and she gave him a hint of a nod. Then she realized that subtlety was unnecessary because Amanda was paying her no attention at all.

"That's silly," Amanda said, frowning. "I've heard those stories, too, but I don't believe them. The people at Top Flight Artists are interested in me, too, but nobody's ever threatened me."

"No kidding?" Ned asked. "How did Top Flight approach you?"

"They called," she said with a smug grin. "Twice. The first time it was an assistant, and then Marty himself. *And* he wrote a note, saying he hoped I'd think about their offer very seriously."

"Are you considering it?" Ned asked.

Amanda looked around to make sure no JZA agents were within earshot. "Maybe," she replied. "You have to look out for yourself, right?"

As Freddy and Jane emerged from the office, Tina Grayce entered the reception area.

"Let's go," Freddy said, opening the door and waving Ned and Amanda toward the elevators.

"Tina," Jane said cheerfully as she took her arm, "Ned has just signed with JZA."

"Really?" Tina stared at Ned. "Great."

"And he landed the very first commercial he was tested for," Jane added proudly.

"Congratulations." Tina looked impressed.

"We'd better be off," Freddy said. Waving goodbye, he shooed Amanda and Ned out the door.

Nancy was glad to see Tina. This would give her a chance to find out how the police had reacted to her information. Nancy turned to Jane and Tina. "Can we talk?" she asked.

"Of course," Jane replied, gesturing toward her office.

Inside, Jane sat at her desk, and Nancy and

Tina sat facing her. Nancy was relieved to see that Tina looked less frantic than yesterday.

"How did it go with Lieutenant Antonio?" she asked the thin redhead.

"Okay, I guess," Tina said, looking annoyed. "He made me come to the precinct and give him a statement. I told him everything I told you. Then he asked if I ever saw the anonymous notes, and I told him no. He wanted to know if I ever actually heard Ursula threatened over the phone. I said no. Then he started to glare at me and asked if I had seen or heard the threats from Marty Prince of Top Flight Artists. I said no. Then he frowned and said rumors were no help at all."

Nancy didn't care for the lieutenant's style but made no comment on it. "I'm sure he'll question Marty about the letters and calls. The main thing is, you did what you had to do."

Tina stood up. "I just wanted to let you know that I saw the police."

Jane smiled warmly at Tina. "Thanks for stopping by. By the way, I've got some odd jobs for you this week, say twenty hours. Maybe you can fix that copier again, all right?"

Tina's face brightened for the first time since Nancy had met her. "Sure! I can use the money. I'll check with Holly to see what hours would be best." Then she left.

As Tina closed the door behind her, Jane sighed. "I feel sorry for her sometimes."

"Does Tina have a future in acting?"

"I'm afraid not," Jane answered, leaning back in her chair. "She wants so much to succeed, but her desperation turns people off. Oh, she's done a few small jobs, the kind that wouldn't interest our busier people. And I give her work here whenever I can. She's great with machines. She's always fixing intercoms, cameras, duplicating machines. It's amazing! The girl has talent, but not the kind of talent she wants so badly."

Nancy felt sorry for Tina. "It's a tough business, isn't it?"

"Some people can't handle it," Jane agreed.

"Why do you keep her under contract?"

"She's not under contract. She's registered here, which means we keep her pictures on file, but she's free to sign elsewhere. When you're not signed with an agent, you can register with anyone who'll have you." Jane had begun tapping a pencil nervously on her desktop. "So, what do you plan to do next as far as this case is concerned?"

"I'd like to look through Ursula's place—if the police haven't sealed it off."

Jane looked doubtful. "The lieutenant won't be happy if he finds out. Does that worry you?"

"I'll try to avoid him, but I can't do much if I'm not willing to risk crossing his path."

"I suppose not," Jane said, flipping through her Rolodex and jotting down a few lines. "Here's her address. She has—*had*—a pretty little place in North Beach. I'll give you directions."

Thirty minutes later, Nancy was squeezing through the narrow streets of North Beach, following Jane's instructions. She parked in front of a white stucco building set on the side of a hill. Nancy climbed the stairs to the third floor, hoping that Ursula hadn't believed in tricky locks.

She reached the third floor landing and saw with a jolt that the door wasn't locked at all. In fact, it stood ajar. Someone had gotten there first. If the police had sealed the apartment, the seal was gone. Someone else had been there, someone not authorized to enter.

The intruder might still be inside!

Standing motionless, she listened carefully for a full minute. The apartment was silent. Very slowly, she pushed the door open.

She looked into a cozy living room, well furnished but now in disarray. Books had been tossed from shelves and lay strewn across the floor. The drawers of a desk stood open, and papers were scattered everywhere. Careful not to touch any of the clutter, Nancy checked the rest of the apartment. Whoever had been here was gone. Had the person found what he or she was looking for?

Nancy closed the apartment door and quickly began looking for hiding places that the first searcher might have missed. She checked under drawers and tables and searched the pockets of Ursula's coats, but found nothing.

In the bedroom, Nancy spent another ten minutes searching. Then she caught her reflection in a heavy mirror hanging over the bureau. Lifting the mirror's carved frame away from the wall, Nancy probed behind it. Something was attached to the backing! She pried loose a manila envelope that had been taped on.

Nancy examined the contents. On top was a note, typed in capital letters on plain paper, which read, "Put your name on the line, or put your life on the line." There was no signature. Other typed notes were equally menacing. Some of the letters, which were handwritten on gray parchment paper, had "From the desk of Marty Prince" printed on top. The notes urged Ursula to meet him, saying that it would be to her advantage.

Nancy replaced the notes in the envelope and returned it to its hiding place. The police would certainly find it when they looked. A blinking light on a bedside table caught her eye. Ursula's answering machine had unplayed messages on it.

She pressed the playback button, and a man's voice came on, hoarse and desperate: "Ursula, I have to see you. I can't go on without you. Please, call me. *Please!*"

There was a beep, and then another voice, this one businesslike: "Ursula, it's Marty. Call me when you can."

That must be Marty Prince, Nancy figured.

Another beep, and then the first voice was back, but this time it sounded ugly: "Who do you think you are? You can't treat me like this. You'll be sorry—you just wait!"

There were no other messages.

The kitchen was undisturbed. A wastebasket with a pedal-operated lid stood by the sink. Nancy pushed the pedal and peered in. Nested in crumpled paper was a large object. Taking a handkerchief, Nancy reached down and picked it up.

It was a mallet with a ten-inch handle and a broad, flat head of heavy, hard wood banded with metal. It didn't look like a kitchen tool. Carved on the handle was the letter S. Nancy looked more closely at the head. It was scarred and battered from heavy use. There was a brown stain on one end. Could be blood, she thought. She replaced the mallet in the wastebasket.

Nancy knew the police would be showing up soon. It was time to get out. She crossed the apartment, opened the door—and leaped backward.

A hulking man stood in the shadows. His legs were planted wide, his arms crossed. Nancy backed away hastily. The man's face was twisted into an ugly scowl. His light blue eyes bored into her with a nasty mixture of suspicion and anger.

"Who are you?" he growled. "And what are you doing in my girlfriend's apartment?"

Chapter

Six

THE BURLY MAN stepped in and closed the door. Nancy swallowed hard. She recognized his voice from the answering machine—he was Sean McKearn, Ursula's ex-boyfriend. He was six feet tall and muscular. His jeans were grimy, and the rolled-up sleeves of his denim shirt revealed brawny forearms. His brown hair was unkempt, and he hadn't shaved in days. He had an aura of barely suppressed violence that set Nancy's nerves on edge. She fought to stay cool and composed.

"I asked you a question," he demanded. Looking past Nancy, he saw the scattered papers and books, and his hands clenched into fists.

"You've ransacked the place!" he growled. "What are you, some kind of thief?"

When Nancy didn't answer, he grabbed her

wrist. His grip was like an iron vise, and pain shot through her arm. "Start talking!"

"Take it easy," Nancy said, trying not to show pain or fear. "The apartment was like this when I got here, and the door was open."

Nancy tried to pull free, but he was too strong. From the way his nostrils flared she sensed anger building up in him. Better be careful, she thought. Out of the corner of her eye, she noticed a heavy glass paperweight on the coffee table. Maybe she could use it as a weapon.

"Be cool, Sean," she urged. "You don't want more trouble."

He dropped her arm and stared, head tilted to one side. "How do you know my name?"

"I heard that Ursula used to date a guy named Sean," she explained cautiously.

Pain replaced the anger in Sean's face. "All that stuff about us breaking up was just temporary. She'd have come back. How do you know so much? Are you a cop?"

"No, I . . ." Her voice trailed off as she realized Sean wasn't listening. He had begun to pace the living room like a caged animal.

"The cops were all over me this morning," he muttered. "Did you sic them on me?"

Having worked himself into a rage again, he whirled toward Nancy, who braced herself for an attack. When he took a swift step toward her she lunged for the paperweight.

"She didn't lead us to you, McKearn," came a new voice. The burly young man spun around, and Nancy dropped the paperweight as she spotted Lieutenant Antonio in the doorway.

"Your winning personality makes you a natural suspect," the lieutenant said. He looked around the room, noticing the disarray and shaking his head. His lips tightened into a thin line. "Playing detective, were you, Ms. Drew?"

"I didn't do this," Nancy stated firmly.

"You're in the apartment of the victim of a violent crime," Antonio said. "Doesn't your amateur detective's handbook warn against messing up evidence in a police investigation?"

"I know it looks bad—" she began.

The lieutenant held up a hand to stop her. "You," he said to Sean. "Out. Beat it, before I haul you in on a trespassing charge."

Sean glared at Nancy for a moment, then stormed out.

Antonio closed the door behind him and turned to Nancy. "We sealed this place last night."

"The door was open when I got here, and the place was trashed," she explained. "I didn't do it."

Lieutenant Antonio's steely look didn't soften. "I told you not to get in my way."

"Jane Zachary asked for my help. She's worried that her clients are being pressured—"

49

"By Marty Prince," the policeman finished. "I got that angle from Jane Zachary yesterday. But it's all rumor, nothing concrete."

Nancy decided that total cooperation might put her in a better light and deflect the lieutenant's anger. She decided to come clean.

"I may as well tell you, I had a look around," she admitted. "I didn't disturb anything and I was careful not to leave prints. But I found a few things of interest."

She took him into the kitchen and pointed out the mallet in the trash. The lieutenant took it out and studied it, holding it delicately with a cloth. He peered at the brown stain.

"It might be blood," Nancy suggested.

He nodded. "The lab will run a test on it."

She showed him the envelope behind the mirror. Taking out the notes, he read them, then tossed them on the bed and shook his head.

"What does this prove?" he asked. "There are some signed notes from Prince and some anonymous threats. Where's the connection?"

Nancy shrugged. "Ursula must have thought there was a connection. She kept them together."

Antonio pulled out a pocket notebook and jotted a few lines. "All right. I'll get samples of Marty Prince's handwriting to compare with the handwritten notes. And we can see if any typewriters at Top Flight match the print on the anonymous notes."

He led Nancy to the front door. "The forensic

team is on its way here. They would've been here sooner, but they're shorthanded this week. My point is, this apartment is off limits to civilians, including you. Is that clear?"

Nancy nodded, adding, "I told Jane Zachary and Evan Chandler that I'd try to find out why JZA is losing clients. That's my focus, not Ursula Biemann. I don't know if there's a connection. But if I do come across anything you should know, I'll call you right away. Will that do?"

The lieutenant sighed. "For my money, Jane Zachary is crazy to bring in an amateur for a case like this. But that's her affair. Now, let me get on with my job."

Nancy returned to Jane Zachary Associates, hoping to find Ned and have lunch. Several good-looking guys were in the reception area, all in checked shirts and jeans. The receptionist called to her, holding out a message.

It was from Ned. He'd called from the wardrobe designer's to say that he was going straight to the photographer's studio, then on to another audition. He would meet Nancy back at Laurel and Evan's house that evening.

Nancy crumpled the note. The vacation wasn't working out as she'd hoped. Ned's life had suddenly become very full, and she wasn't a part of it. She had thought that having Ned work on this case would help to bring them together. Instead, it was keeping them apart.

"Who's next for the Rancho Chips commercial?" Evan called from the doorway. Nancy saw one of the guys in western gear stand up just as Evan noticed her. "Hey, Nancy. You get Ned's message?"

"Right here," she said, holding up the paper.

Evan lowered his voice. "You asked about Nelson Taylor, the guy Sean tangled with? That's him." He pointed to a guy with wavy black hair and blue eyes, which were fixed on Nancy. He grinned at her, showing off his even teeth.

Evan beckoned, and Nelson joined them. "Nancy Drew, meet Nelson Taylor. Nelson, would you mind talking to Nancy for a few minutes?"

"Would I mind talking to a beautiful girl? No problem," Nelson said, flashing her a brilliant smile and tossing back his hair. This guy is too vain for words, Nancy thought.

"Use my office," Evan suggested.

Trying to be gracious, Nancy led Nelson to Evan's office. As she closed the door, Nelson leaned against the desk.

"You must be new around here," he said. "If I'd seen you before, I'd definitely remember."

"I'm just visiting. I was wondering—"

"Do you want my special guided tour of the city?" Nelson strolled over to her, thumbs hooked in his belt loops. "We'd have a blast! I know this cozy restaurant where we could—"

"I don't think so, thanks. My boyfriend would feel left out," Nancy said. Ignoring Nelson's sigh, she added, "I hear you got into a scrape with Sean McKearn over Ursula Biemann."

"That dude." Nelson scowled. "He's crazy, you know? Ursula and I, we just worked together. Not that I'd have minded dating her, but she wasn't interested. I wished her happy holidays at a party, and Sean blew a fuse. I'd have decked him right then, but I didn't want to upset people."

Nancy doubted that Nelson could have taken Sean on, but she didn't comment. "So you didn't provoke Sean? You weren't making a play for Ursula?"

"I don't have to steal girls," he insisted. "I do fine on my own. No, it was innocent, and only a nut case like Sean would think different."

"Has Marty Prince ever been in touch with you?" Nancy asked. "This is just between us."

Nelson's smile vanished as if he'd flipped a switch. "I won't talk about him. He's bad news."

"Did he ask you to sign with Top Flight?"

"Yeah, but I turned him down. He tried again and I said no. Then—no, forget it. That Marty has sharp ears and long arms, you know?"

"It's important," Nancy urged. "Could you just give me some idea of—"

"I said no!" Nelson snapped. "I usually cooperate with gorgeous women, but I want to stay healthy and handsome for a while. Understand?"

Nancy nodded. "Thanks for your time."

Nelson's brilliant smile returned. "Listen," he

cooed, "if you and your boyfriend ever break up, that tour offer is always available."

Not a chance, Nancy thought as she thanked him and ducked out of the room. She went to Jane's office, where Jane and Evan were waiting.

"Any progress?" Jane asked.

"I checked out Ursula's place." Nancy glanced at her watch. She felt ravenously hungry. "Have you two eaten yet?"

Evan picked up the hint. "Why don't we have lunch?" he suggested. "I'm starved, myself. We can introduce Nancy to Mimi's. They have the best seafood at Fisherman's Wharf. We'll talk there."

Soon Nancy was sitting over a steaming bowl of clam chowder in a glass-enclosed dining room overlooking the blue bay. Taking a hunk of crusty sourdough bread from a basket, she described what she had found at Ursula's place, and her encounters with Sean and the lieutenant.

"Can you tell me more about Sean and his fights with Ursula?" Nancy asked Evan. She bit into the bread, which was warm and delicious.

"He's a sculptor who's never been able to sell anything, so he makes his living as a carpenter," Evan said, then took a spoonful of his chowder. "He had a hard time accepting the fact that Ursula was more successful than he was. Right, Jane?"

Jane nodded agreement, her fork poised over a salad. "Also, he couldn't stand her working with good-looking guys. That was what started the fight at the Christmas party."

"You don't know anything about why he was arrested?" Nancy asked.

Jane and Evan shook their heads. Nancy resolved to find out more about the arrest. "I'd really like to meet Marty Prince," she said, "if I can figure out a good excuse."

Just then a waiter whisked away Evan's bowl, replacing it with a main course.

Evan beamed. "Aah, abalone. Ever try it?"

Nancy laughed. "I think I'm about to."

"That's right," Evan said, giving her a piece. "Oh, about dinner tonight. Laurel suggested that the four of us try a German restaurant on Telegraph Hill. Good food. Tramway ride. How about it?"

"It sounds fine," Nancy said. A romantic dinner might be just what she and Ned needed.

After lunch, Nancy drove to a shopping district Laurel had mentioned, on Union Street. But even the funky boutiques couldn't put her in a shopping mood. So she arrived back at the Chandlers' house by midafternoon.

She went through her clothes, looking for exactly the right outfit to wear that evening, and settled on a soft sheath of deep purple. She laid it on the bed and looked out the window. A white curtain of fog was coming in off the Pacific, already hiding the bridge. Hearing a car pull up, Nancy glanced down at the street below.

A cute red convertible with the top down had parked in front of the house. Ned sat in the passenger seat, laughing and animated.

The driver was Amanda.

Nancy wanted to turn away. She felt as if she were spying on Ned. But she stood there, rooted, watching Ned and Amanda chat.

They look as if they're in a commercial right now, she thought.

Then, as Ned started to reach for the door, Amanda leaned across, slipped her hands over his shoulders, and kissed him on the lips.

Chapter

Seven

NANCY TURNED AWAY, feeling a wrenching pain in the pit of her stomach. She sat on the bed, uncertain about what to do. Downstairs, the front door opened and closed, and she heard Ned speak. Then Laurel called up from the foot of the stairs.

"Nancy! Ned's back."

"Coming!" Nancy called. She decided to say nothing to Ned. She hated the notion of looking jealous, even if that was how she felt. Anyway, the kiss just proved that Amanda was attracted to Ned. It didn't mean Ned was interested in Amanda—did it?

Ned was sitting at one end of the long, over-stuffed living room couch when Nancy met him downstairs. Across from him, Laurel was pouring iced tea from a pitcher.

"What's this I hear about another audition?" Nancy said, crossing the room.

"Don't get too excited." Ned took a glass from Laurel as Nancy sat next to him. "The audition was a waste of time. They wanted a guy who would fit into this giant plastic bleach bottle, and I was too tall."

Laughing, Laurel handed Nancy a glass. "A giant bleach bottle? Evan tells me stories like that, but I always find them hard to believe."

"And those head shots," Ned added. "Now *that* was a hassle. They took forever to set up the lights, and then the photographer started fussing with my hair and my clothes. The lights were so hot, it felt as if I were being microwaved."

Nancy shook her head sympathetically. "And you were in that wool blazer, too."

Ned nodded. "Finally they started shooting, and they took hundreds of shots—with my jacket on, with it off, with my tie loosened and my collar open, sitting, standing, smiling, looking serious." Ned demonstrated his expressions, getting giggles from Laurel and Nancy.

"Have any trouble getting back here?" Nancy asked.

"No problem," Ned said. "I got a ride."

Nancy took a sip of iced tea, waiting for Ned to mention Amanda, maybe even joke about how she made a play for him and how he set her straight. But he said nothing further.

"Did you get any information?" Nancy asked.

"Information?" His face was blank.

"You know," Nancy said. "About Top Flight or Marty Prince or actors getting threatened?"

"Oh." Ned looked a little embarrassed. "No, not really. Everything was so hectic—I just didn't have the chance to bring it up. Sorry."

"It's all right," Nancy replied, not meeting Ned's eyes. He had obviously forgotten what he was supposed to do. Was it because he had been so caught up with what he was doing with Amanda?

A few minutes later Evan arrived, and Nancy went upstairs to change for dinner. As she slipped on her purple dress, she realized that Ned hadn't asked how her day had gone. Was he so wrapped up in Amanda and his new career that he'd lost interest in Nancy? There was only one thing that Nancy was sure of: Something was wrong.

The tram ride up the mountain was a fun way to begin the evening. Once they arrived at the top of the hill, Nancy was glad to get out of the night air and step into the warm, cozy restaurant.

A rustic mountain cabin perched on a rocky shoulder of Telegraph Hill, the restaurant provided stunning views on all sides. The lights of San Francisco stretched below like ribbons of jewels. The dining area was very homey and pleasant, with low-ceilinged, half-timbered rooms and a gigantic hearth in which a fire crackled.

Evan's and Laurel's sunny humor had a warming effect on Nancy and Ned. Before long they had loosened up, laughing and enjoying Evan's anecdotes about his work and Laurel's stories about Ned when he was little. Finally beginning to relax, Ned reached for Nancy's hand and held it while they waited for dessert. Nancy started to feel better about how things stood between them.

As they dug into rich pastries, Laurel turned the conversation to Nancy. "Evan says that you found some clues in that model's apartment today."

Nancy told Ned and Laurel about what she'd found in Ursula's apartment. "I don't know what it means. As Lieutenant Antonio pointed out, the threats were anonymous and the notes signed by Marty were innocent. The fact that they were all in one envelope is suggestive, but not incriminating."

"What about the card in Ursula's purse?" Evan asked. "Doesn't that mean something?"

Nancy sighed. "Marty must have given out thousands of cards. It's not a crime for him to have given one to Ursula." She frowned. "Actually, that card does bother me, but I don't know exactly what to make of it."

"I'd bet anything that Marty Prince is guilty," Laurel insisted.

Evan smiled fondly at his wife. "Too bad intuition isn't evidence, honey." He turned to Ned. "One thing's for sure, you're going to come out of this with some nice photos of yourself. Mario is the best photographer in the city."

Ned smiled. "Boy, I hope you're right. That session was a killer. I thought it'd never end, what with all the lights to be adjusted. And then, once he started shooting, it was all I could do to keep a straight face, with Amanda mugging at me and clowning around behind Mario's back—"

"Amanda?" Nancy asked. "You mean she went to the photo session, too? Not just the fitting?"

"Sure," Ned replied. "Didn't I tell you? Freddy couldn't drive me to the studio, so Amanda volunteered. She said she had some free time—"

"How nice of her," Nancy said, more harshly than she had meant to. A little voice in the back of her head told her to let it go and not make a scene, but she wasn't sure she could.

"That's right," he said, giving Nancy a cool look. "Amanda gave me tips about how to get the best results when you're photographed, and it *was* nice of her. She drove me home, too. She did me a favor, and we had a few laughs." He stuck out his hands. "Put the cuffs on me, Officer, I'll come along quietly."

He grinned, as if the whole exchange had been a joke, but Nancy was upset. She let the subject

61

drop, but there was an awkward silence at the table. Evan finally broke it by asking for the check.

The cozy atmosphere was ruined. Nancy wished that she could turn back the clock and do the last fifteen minutes over again. Whatever was wrong between her and Ned, she knew she had handled it badly and made the situation worse. Neither Evan nor Laurel tried to start up a conversation as they rode the tram back to where they had parked.

As Evan started the car, Laurel touched her husband's arm. "Don't forget, you have to stop by the agency."

"Oh, right," Evan said. "Thanks, honey." He twisted around to face the backseat, where Ned and Nancy sat in awkward silence. "Mind if we swing by JZA? I promised Jane that I'd look at some photos tonight, and I left them on my desk."

"No problem," Nancy said softly.

Ned just nodded.

As they rode, Nancy tried to think of something to say to lighten the mood, but her mind was blank. Now and then she glanced over at Ned, hoping to catch his eye and end the standoff. But he stared ahead, his jaw set, his expression distant. Although they were only inches apart on the car seat, to Nancy it felt like miles.

Finally, after what seemed to be hours, they pulled up in front of the JZA building.

"I won't bother using the garage," Evan said, throwing open the door. "It'll just be a minute." He stepped out, stopped abruptly, and sniffed the air. "Do you smell smoke?"

Nancy rolled down her window, and instantly she could smell that there was a fire nearby. "You're right," she replied. "Something's burning."

Quickly, Nancy, Laurel, and Ned got out of the car and looked around.

"I see it!" Ned exclaimed, pointing up at the building.

Nancy looked up at one of the upper stories, where smoke was billowing out of a vent.

"That's our floor!" Evan shouted. "Come on!" He broke into a run, and the others followed.

"Don't use the elevators!" Ned shouted as they stormed into the lobby.

Evan led the way to the stairs and raced up, taking the steps two at a time.

With gritted teeth, Nancy pushed herself to keep up with him.

The first one to reach the agency's floor, Evan threw open the stairwell door and dashed into the hall. Nancy and Ned were right on his heels, and Laurel followed close behind.

JZA shared the floor with one other company. Both firms were entered by way of double glass doors across the hall from each other. Panting slightly when he came to a dead stop in front of the JZA doors, Evan stared in horror. Nancy and Ned ran up behind him, then froze, transfixed by the sight.

Flames enveloped the furniture and streaked along the walls. Fire was raging through the agency, destroying everything!

Chapter

Eight

Evan started forward, but Nancy quickly reached out and grabbed his arm.

"No!" she shouted. "You can't go in there, it's out of control!"

Evan seemed stunned, almost hypnotized. He pulled away from Nancy's grip, insisting, "There are important papers—"

"Evan! No!" Laurel screamed. "It's not worth dying for." She coughed as acrid fumes seeped between the doors.

"Let's get out of here," Ned yelled, putting a hand on Evan's shoulder. "The heat of the fire could blow those glass doors out."

Evan suddenly looked drained and defeated. "This'll ruin us," he said dully.

"Let's find a phone and call it in. Maybe you

THE NANCY DREW FILES

can salvage something." Nancy's voice was raspy, her throat raw and aching from the smoke.

"There are phones in the lobby. I'll call the fire department!" Laurel yelled, running to the stairwell.

"Come on!" Ned shouted. He and Nancy took Evan by the arms and tugged.

The agent hung back, taking a last despairing look at JZA before allowing himself to be pulled out of the hall.

Just as the door to the stairwell closed, Nancy heard a sharp crashing noise.

"There go the glass doors," Ned said. "Good thing we got out of there."

They arrived in the lobby as Laurel gave JZA's address to the dispatcher on the other end of the phone. "Please hurry," she added before hanging up.

Ned pushed open the outside doors, and they scrambled through. For a minute no one spoke as they concentrated on soothing their lungs and throats with deep breaths of cool night air.

"I don't get it," Evan said, coughing. "We have a sprinkler system and fire alarms. Why didn't they cut in? I'd better call Jane."

As he went into the lobby, sirens wailed through the nearby streets. Moments later a hook-and-ladder rig swung around the corner and stopped. Two other trucks and a car, all bright red, pulled up, and more than a dozen fire fighters piled out to attack the blaze.

Evan returned. "Jane's on her way," he said.

Ten minutes later, Jane drove up. From her faded jeans and a shaggy sweater, Nancy could see that she had dressed in a hurry. She was a far cry from the picture of elegance she normally presented. Walking up to the others, Jane nodded. "How bad is it?"

With his arm around Laurel's shoulders, Evan looked despondent. "The front room was engulfed in flames," he said. "The smoke was too thick to really see."

"You have insurance, don't you?" Nancy asked.

"Of course," Jane said, sounding strained and edgy. "But there are a lot of things here that will be very hard to replace, like clients' photos and résumés. If we lose our phone lines, we can't do business. This couldn't have come at a worse time, just when—"

"Excuse me," said a voice behind her. A young man in a suit and tinted glasses held out a gold badge in a leather case. "Inspector Ken Matsuda, S.F.F.D. Who called in the fire?"

Evan identified himself and explained what had happened, while the inspector took notes. At one point, a firefighter interrupted and took the inspector aside for a brief conference. Then Matsuda returned.

"It's lucky you came by, Mr. Chandler," he said. "Otherwise, the entire floor would be a burnt-out shell. As it is, I think that several rooms in back are usable."

Jane came forward. "It's not a total loss?"

"And you are—?" the inspector said.

"Jane Zachary," she said. "It's my agency. Can we go up and check the damage?"

"If you like. There's no danger now," said Inspector Matsuda. "We can talk afterward. But be careful. The floors are wet and slippery."

The elevators had been shut down, so everyone trudged up the stairs, passing fire fighters who were on their way down. When they reached JZA's floor, Nancy's eyes began to tear from the acrid smoke, and she noticed an awful, charred smell.

"You'll need these," the inspector said as he handed flashlights to Jane and Evan. "The lights are out."

Nancy stood with Jane in the doorway and surveyed the dismal remains of what had been a stylish office suite. The flashlight beams swept over puddles of water and piles of ashes.

In Jane's office the beautiful carpet and the antique furniture were scorched, drenched, and ruined. Jane took a wad of soggy paper from her desk. Nancy saw they had once been an actor's head shots, with résumés printed on the backs. Wordlessly, Jane dropped them on the floor. Nancy noted that Jane showed no signs of emotion.

The inspector waved them back out to the hallway. "I have a few more questions," he said.

"How did it happen?" Jane asked.

"It's too soon to say," Matsuda responded. "Ms. Zachary, were your alarms and sprinklers in working order?"

"As far as I know," she replied quietly.

The inspector made a notation. "Who handles your insurance?"

Jane blinked. "Why do you ask?"

"Standard procedure," he replied. "I imagine you'll call them right away."

"Oh." Jane stared straight ahead, motionless as a statue. Nancy thought that she might be in shock. There was no sign of distress at all. "Yes, I'll call tonight." She gave him the name of her insurance agent. "Will that be all?"

Inspector Matsuda closed his notebook. "For now. We may need to talk again. I've still got a few things to check out here." He nodded, then walked back into the devastated agency.

Does he suspect foul play? Nancy wondered.

Jane turned to Evan. "First thing in the morning, we'll set up temporary headquarters."

"Sure thing," Evan said, squeezing Jane's hands. "It could have been worse. We'll manage, you'll see."

Jane smiled weakly. Then a hard look came into her eyes as she said, "I suppose Marty Prince will be sorry to hear his plan didn't work."

Laurel gasped. "You think *he* did this?"

Jane looked back at the agency. "Let's just say I wouldn't put it past him."

Nancy thought Jane was assuming too much. "First, let's see if the fire was arson," she said. "It might have been a freak accident, like a short circuit, or a wiring—"

Jane turned to face Nancy. "You don't really think that, do you? I'll bet it was arson, and if it was, then I know who's responsible. See you in the morning, Evan." She walked out the door.

"She sure was cool under the circumstances," Laurel commented.

"Maybe she was too stunned to react," Nancy suggested, though she agreed with Laurel. Jane's unusual calm had brought a few questions to mind.

How shaky was JZA financially? Had Top Flight Artists threatened JZA's existence? Was Jane Zachary desperate enough to try to collect the insurance money by arranging to burn down her own business?

Nancy had a night of restless sleep and nightmares. In one dream she stood at the edge of a wall of fire, shouting to Ned, who stood on the opposite side, obscured by smoke and flames. But no matter how many times she called, he never heard.

The next morning she was on her way down to breakfast when she heard Ned's voice in the kitchen. "Ever since she got back from Europe, things have been messed up. Now she's acting suspicious and possessive."

Nancy stopped and listened, her heart pounding. The next voice she heard was Laurel's.

"I could tell there was something wrong. Is it serious, do you think?"

Afraid to hear Ned's reply, Nancy came down the stairs, making noise so they'd hear her. As she expected, the conversation broke off. They looked up as she walked in, Laurel with a smile fixed in place, Ned with a sad expression.

"Good morning," Nancy said, feeling self-conscious.

"Can I fix you some pancakes?" Laurel offered. "I made some for Ned. Poor Evan had to get up at dawn to head down to the agency."

"No, thanks." Nancy popped a slice of bread into the toaster. "I'm not too hungry."

Ned stood up, and Nancy noticed he was wearing a sweatsuit and running shoes. "Guess I'll run a few miles. See you later." He nodded at Nancy and walked quickly out of the kitchen.

Ordinarily he would have asked me to join him, Nancy thought sadly. But not today. Tears stung her eyes as she sat down at the table.

Laurel sat opposite Nancy, looking at her with concern. "Are you all right?" she asked.

"I've been better." The toast popped up, but Nancy ignored it. "I guess you know things are strained between Ned and me."

"I feel bad for you both." Laurel put her hand over Nancy's. Her look of concern warmed Nancy. "What's the problem?"

Though Nancy wasn't sure where to begin, she filled Laurel in on their summer apart, and on the feelings she'd been having since they'd arrived in San Francisco. "It's not just that I'm jealous of Amanda," Nancy said. "If Ned pursues a modeling career, it will pull us further apart. I just don't know if Ned and I really belong together."

Laurel listened intently before she spoke. "Don't be so hard on yourself," she said, smiling. "Jealousy isn't such a terrible thing. It proves that you really do care about Ned."

"I hadn't looked at it that way," Nancy said thoughtfully.

"As for Ned's glamorous new career," Laurel added, "my cousin is a sensible guy. His head may be spinning from all the attention he's been getting, but he'll sort things out."

"I hope so, because I can't—" The doorbell cut Nancy off. Laurel excused herself to answer the door. She came back a moment later, carrying a folded piece of gray paper.

"Someone just pushed this through the mail slot," she said. "It's for Ned."

Nancy looked at the paper—a gray parchment that seemed familiar. Suddenly she remembered. It resembled the notes in Ursula's apartment.

"Can I see it?" Nancy asked.

Laurel looked doubtful. "I don't know," she murmured. "I mean, it *is* addressed to Ned."

Nancy understood Laurel's reluctance. "I have a strong hunch that it might connect with my case," Nancy explained, "otherwise I wouldn't think of looking at it. Really."

Laurel bit her lip. At length she said, "Well . . . all right," and handed over the note.

Nancy opened it up. The brief message was handwritten: "We should talk right away. Give me a call."

There was a phone number written below. The same name was signed at the bottom of the note and printed at the top—Marty Prince.

Chapter

Nine

READING THE MESSAGE, Nancy felt her sad feelings over Ned give way to a stir of excitement. Marty Prince hadn't wasted any time.

Laurel read over Nancy's shoulder. "How did he hear about Ned so quickly?" she asked.

"That's a good question," Nancy said. "And how did he know where Ned is staying?"

Laurel gasped. "That's right!"

Nancy stood up and began to pace. "I've been looking for a way to meet Marty and here it is." She had felt the case stalling for lack of direction. Now at least she had a plan.

"I'm not sure that's such a good idea," Laurel cautioned. "He could be dangerous."

Nancy nodded. "Evan says he's clever," she said. "He'll take some careful handling."

Suddenly hungry, she ate a hearty breakfast

74

while waiting for Ned to return. The minute he came in the door, she handed him the note, explaining, "It was delivered while you were out."

Ned quickly scanned it. "How does Marty Prince know about me?"

"Let's find out. Give him a call and set up an appointment," Nancy suggested.

"This morning I have to go try on the King Kola wardrobe," Ned said thoughtfully. "Freddy and Amanda are meeting me there in an hour. I could see Marty afterward."

"Great," Nancy said. "I'll go with you."

"Why?" Ned scowled. "Because you don't trust me alone with Amanda?"

Stung, Nancy tried to keep resentment out of her voice. "It has nothing to do with Amanda. I just want to meet Marty Prince. If you want, I'll meet you after you're done with your wardrobe."

Ned looked away, muttering, "I'm sorry. I guess I jumped to the wrong conclusion."

"It's all right," Nancy replied. "Maybe we've both been doing too much of that lately." Catching his attention, she smiled and was happy to see a glimmer of warmth in his eyes.

"Maybe we have," Ned agreed. "I'll call Top Flight right now." He dialed, and once he gave his name, Marty got on the line immediately. By the time Ned hung up, he had arranged to meet Marty in his office at one o'clock that afternoon.

"He wants to make me a star," Ned said, chuckling.

"Nice work, Nickerson," Nancy said, then glanced away. "So what's the plan?" she asked casually. "Should I meet you after your fitting?"

"No—come along," Ned insisted. "Just let me shower and change."

Nancy went to her room and looked through her closet. She put on a royal blue top and slinky black leggings. Studying herself in the mirror, she smiled. If Amanda wants Ned, she thought, she'll have to deal with me first.

Ned drove them to the production company in the Mission District, near where Ursula Biemann's body had been found. Freddy Estevez was waiting for them, and he trotted over as Ned parked the car.

"Right on time, Ned," Freddy said, leading them into a room cluttered with props and lights. "Amanda's trying her stuff on already, and she looks fantastic."

Wonderful, Nancy thought, but kept quiet.

Nancy noticed big cue cards stacked against the wall. The giant print on the cards made her crack a smile as she walked by. "Don't suffer the heartache of heartburn!" said one card. On another she read: "My mom is the greatest 'cause she gives us Choco-Yums for dessert!"

"Here we are," Freddy said, as they entered a room with racks full of colorful clothes: sequined circus tights, ornate brocade dresses and crinolines, and even a Mountie uniform. Paper tags with Ned's name were pinned to a few hangers.

"Try this on first," Freddy said, handing Ned an outfit. "It's for the balloon sequence. Use the second dressing room." He pointed to some doors in the far wall. Ned nodded and smiled at Nancy as he went into the cubicle marked number two.

As he did, door number one opened and out came Amanda, frowning. Nancy thought she looked like someone from a dude ranch or a western movie. She wore stiff new jeans and a checkered blouse with pearl buttons. A mini-cowboy hat was perched on the back of her head.

"This is really dumb," Amanda pouted. "Freddy, can't they change this?"

"You look adorable," Freddy insisted. "And it goes with Ned's outfit. Besides, you'll be up in that hot-air balloon. You need a costume that will come across from a distance."

When Ned came out with an embarrassed smirk, Nancy had to bite her lip to keep a straight face. He *did* look like a match for Amanda. He too wore starchy new jeans, and his western-style shirt had little bucking horses all over it. In his hand he held a ten-gallon hat.

"Do I have to wear this thing?" he asked.

Freddy nodded. "You and Amanda will look great together. A modern couple having a fun weekend and drinking King Kola."

Groaning, Ned put on the hat, and Nancy

couldn't hold back a yelp of laughter. Ned looked foolish and knew it. He gave Nancy a mock scowl.

"Hey, cowboy," Amanda said brightly as Ned spotted her.

"Howdy, ma'am," Ned drawled, tipping his enormous hat. "You kin call me Tex."

Amanda giggled. "Howdy, Tex. Maybe we'll be lucky and no one will recognize us in this stuff."

"Why, shucks, ma'am," Ned replied. "I think you look plumb fine in that rig. You're one right purty heifer."

As Amanda collapsed in laughter, Nancy felt her new hopes for her relationship with Ned begin to drain away. The sight of the two of them clowning and cutting up together made her feel as though they were more like a couple than she and Ned.

Nancy sank back onto a clothes trunk and waited quietly while Ned and Amanda tried on the other outfits. Ned kept up a steady stream of cracks, which Amanda found hilarious. He seemed to genuinely like Amanda and enjoy her company. As for Amanda, it was obvious to Nancy that she thought Ned was terrific.

"You two are going to look perfect tomorrow," Freddy said when the fitting was finished. The wiry man clapped Ned on the back. "I'll leave a message at the Chandlers' telling where and when to report tomorrow. It'll be early, I'm afraid. We have to be on location in Napa Valley by seven-thirty."

"I'll be there," Ned assured him.

Amanda draped an emerald green scarf over her shoulders and said to Ned, "See you in the morning, Tex."

"Afternoon, ma'am," Ned drawled, winking.

As they drove to Top Flight Artists, Nancy tried to find something to say, but words wouldn't come. They rode in silence for a while, until Ned pulled up at a red light and turned toward her.

"You have a real problem with Amanda, don't you?" he said gently. "The thing is, she's kind of sweet."

"I can see she's sweet on *you,* anyway," Nancy said, feeling her face heat up with emotion.

"You don't trust me," Ned said, slapping the steering wheel in frustration. "You sat there the whole time I was kidding around with Amanda and didn't crack a smile. It's getting embarrassing."

"The light's green," Nancy said. She knew there was some truth in Ned's words, but she still wasn't ready to talk about her jealous feelings—and her concerns that she and Ned were growing apart.

She reached out and touched his cheek. "Ned, you're right. I *have* been suspicious. I guess I'm having a hard time with your shot at fame."

Ned nodded slowly. "But, Nan," he said earnestly, "I need you to trust me. What's happened to us? I mean, how can you be in love with someone when you don't trust them?"

The question sent a jolt of emotion searing through Nancy. Right now she didn't know how to begin to answer it. Fortunately, she was saved as Ned pulled up in front of a three-story frame building.

"Here we are, Top Flight Artists," he said, backing the car into a spot on the street.

"We'll talk about this later, Ned," Nancy told him.

His handsome face looked sad as he nodded. "Just think about what I said," he told her. "You have to trust me, Nan."

The agency occupied the ground floor of the building. As they got out of the car, Nancy heard arguing voices coming from Top Flight.

Ned stood for a moment with his head cocked, listening. "Someone isn't happy in there."

The words of the quarrel weren't audible, but it involved a man and a woman. The woman's voice grew higher and shriller until the front door to the agency abruptly opened. Then a young woman with flaming red hair burst outside, almost running.

With a shock Nancy recognized Tina Grayce.

Seeing Nancy and Ned, Tina stopped short and stared at them with alarm. She looked as pale and shaken as when Nancy had first seen her.

Nancy wondered what business Tina had with Marty Prince, since Jane Zachary had done so much to help her.

"Tina," Nancy said. "You remember us, don't you? We— Tina, what's the matter?"

The distraught redhead had grabbed Nancy's arm and was pulling her away from the agency door.

"What is it?" Nancy asked. "Are you okay?"

"I don't want him to see or hear us talking," the girl whispered. "He warned me to keep quiet."

"Who did?" Ned asked. "You mean Marty Prince? Was he yelling at you just now?"

Tina nodded. "That was Marty. He left a message with my service last night that he wanted to see me. I'm registered here, and I'd hoped it was an audition. Boy, was I wrong. Marty said he knew I'd told the police about him. He's furious! He said I'd gotten him into a lot of trouble."

"Did he threaten you?" Nancy demanded. "If he did, you should tell the police and—"

"No!" Tina insisted. "No more police. I took your advice before, and look what happened. I'm finished with the police. I don't want to end up in some alley like Ursula."

"Did he mention Ursula?" Nancy took her by the shoulders. "Tina, if he actually threatened you, the police can do something about it. Don't you see?"

Tina pulled loose. "You're the one who doesn't see. Marty wouldn't make an obvious threat. But he makes his meaning very clear."

"What did he tell you?" Ned asked.

Tina took a deep, ragged breath. "He said that terrible things can happen to people who are foolish, like Ursula, and that if I'm smart I'll forget everything I told the police."

Tina shuddered and lowered her voice to a whisper. "Then he said if I didn't follow his advice, the next time my picture got into the papers, it would be on the obituary page."

Chapter

Ten

TINA LOOKED fearfully back over her shoulder. "I'd better go," she said.

"Did anyone else hear this?" Nancy asked.

Tina shook her head. "It's his word against mine. He'll deny saying anything to me at all." She looked from Ned to Nancy and back. "By the way, what are you guys doing here?"

Ned spoke up quickly. "Marty wants to talk. He probably wants me to join his agency."

Tina's eyes narrowed. "Well, just watch out. You can't trust him."

"Tina, one more question—" Nancy began, but the redhead retreated.

"I can't stay," Tina insisted. "It's too risky. If Marty sees us together, I'm dead meat. I'm leaving." She turned on her heel and walked away, not looking back.

"How did Marty know Tina went to the police?" Nancy asked. "Is there a leak in the department?"

"Who else knew she was going?" Ned asked.

Nancy considered the question. "You and me, Evan . . . and Jane."

"Jane?" Ned looked skeptical. "Don't tell me you suspect Jane?"

"I don't know," Nancy admitted. "But think about the insurance money she would have collected if the agency had been a total loss—which it would have been if we hadn't stopped by. And her reaction to the fire was awfully low-key."

"I see what you mean," Ned said thoughtfully.

"It's something to keep in mind," Nancy said as she pushed open the door marked Top Flight Artists.

From the layout of the building, Nancy guessed that the agency's suite had recently been an apartment. The flowered wallpaper and heavy drapes in the front room were holdovers from when it had been used as a living room.

The receptionist, a tall, big-boned blond woman with Nordic looks, took Ned's name and buzzed Marty's office. Seconds later, a short, thin man with a deep tan and curly black hair emerged from a door behind the receptionist's desk. His metal-framed aviator-style glasses were tinted amber, and he wore faded jeans cinched by a wide belt with a silver buckle.

"Ned!" he exclaimed, flashing a smile. "Marty

Prince. It's good of you to come on such short notice. I've heard great things about you." He saw Nancy. "And who's this lovely redhead?"

"Nancy Drew," Ned supplied. "She's visiting San Francisco with me, so she came along."

"Fine, no problem. Come right this way and let's talk." Marty wheeled toward his office door, calling back to the receptionist, "Claire, no calls and no interruptions."

He opened his door and gestured for Nancy and Ned to precede him. Marty's office was small and neat. Instead of a desk, he used an antique table with claw feet. The wall was hung with signed photos of Marty being hugged by other people, presumably actors. Nancy peered at the pictures and recognized a few faces, but none were major stars.

Marty nodded at the photos. "From my Hollywood days," he explained. "I worked at an agency in Tinseltown before I moved here." Turning away from the pictures, he surveyed Ned and clapped his hands. "I see what the fuss was about. You have the look, Ned. And it's unique, you're not just a copy of some other guy. I can do a lot with you."

"I was surprised to get your note," Ned replied. "I mean, we only got here a few days ago, and I had my first audition the day before yesterday. How did you hear about me so fast?"

Marty chuckled and winked. "It's a small city, and this business has its own little grapevine. The minute I heard about you I said to myself, 'Marty, you have to sign this one up.'"

"It's a very efficient grapevine," Nancy commented, "if it told you where we were staying."

"That's why Ned should accept my offer," he said, avoiding a direct response. Marty's smile became a little strained. "I'm new here, and I'm ambitious. When I hear of something I want, I know how to reach out for it. You need a hungry agent, Ned. I'd make sure that you got auditions."

"I don't know," Ned replied. "JZA has treated me well. I got a job my first day. How much more can I expect from an agent than that? Also, Evan Chandler is my cousin-in-law, so I feel a certain loyalty to his people."

Marty tilted his chair back and put his feet on the table. Nancy tried to read his face, but the amber glasses masked his eyes. "Loyalty is a fine thing," he said, "but don't take it too far. You have to go where your best interests lie."

"I'll level with you," Ned said earnestly. "I just signed a contract with JZA."

Marty swung his feet to the floor, and the front legs of his chair dropped with a thud. Nancy detected an unpleasant tightening in the agent's jaw muscles. "I hate to see promising young talent like you make a serious mistake. I'm afraid you're going to regret your decision, Ned."

Was he threatening Ned? Nancy looked intently at the agent. "What do you mean, exactly?" she demanded.

Marty took off his glasses and put them down. Nancy studied his slate-colored eyes.

"JZA is a very shaky operation these days," Marty said. "Jane Zachary's been on thin ice for months—long before last night's fire. And let me tell you, I was shocked and horrified when I heard the news. Sounds to me as if Jane has a law-suit against the people who put in the sprinklers and fire alarms—they should have worked."

How did Marty know all the details of the fire already? Nancy wondered. The information about JZA's fire alarms wasn't public knowledge.

"The point is," Marty summed up, "JZA could go under at any time. And when they do, actors who hesitated to make the smart move will find themselves out in the cold."

"Actors like Tina Grayce?" Nancy asked.

Marty appeared taken aback by the name, but he recovered and shook his head sadly.

"So you met Tina?" He glanced away, adding, "She's an unfortunate girl. I feel sorry for her. She's been begging me to take her as a client, but I had to turn her down. Tina's not very stable. She tends to rant and rave. Today was the all-time worst. She screamed and made crazy threats, told me I'd be sorry, whatever that means."

As he said this, Marty looked sincere. Nancy realized that it could quite possibly be true. Tina was terribly eager to achieve success. And she was certainly capable of making a scene.

"What kind of trouble is JZA in?" she asked.

"Money trouble," Marty said, smiling thinly. "When we started up we lured away some of their most valuable models and actors. We've hurt their business. They've had to make cutbacks."

Nancy already knew this was true from Jane and Evan. Marty was persuasive. Maybe he was also honest. If so, what did that imply about Jane? Was Jane simply wrong about Marty, or was she trying to manipulate Nancy to suspect him?

"And now they've lost another valuable asset," Ned said. "Ursula Biemann."

Marty shook his head. "What a tragedy. But that was *our* loss—not Jane's."

"Your loss? How's that?" Nancy asked.

"Before she died, Ursula decided to switch to Top Flight," Marty said. "As I told the police earlier today, her contract with JZA had almost expired, and she was going to come over here."

Nancy was stunned. If Marty was telling the truth, he wouldn't have wanted anything to happen to Ursula.

"Are you sure?" she asked. "Jane said that Ursula was planning to stay with JZA."

"Just a second," Marty said, going to a file cabinet. Opening a drawer, he pulled out a piece of paper. "Read it," he invited, holding the paper up for Nancy and Ned to glance over.

It was brief, just a paragraph saying that Ursula would sign her next representation contract with Top Flight Artists. Her signature was at the bottom. It hit Nancy like a physical blow. She would have to throw out her basic assumptions about the case. Jane was either mistaken or lying.

"I guess Jane didn't know about Ursula's plans," Ned said.

"I'm not sure," Marty replied. "Ursula said she was going to tell Jane a couple of days ago—the day before she was killed, in fact. I know it would have been a bombshell to Jane, possibly the finishing blow to her business."

Marty got up to replace the document, adding, "Maybe Ursula *did* tell Jane. Maybe Jane lost her temper. Maybe that's why Ursula was killed."

Chapter

Eleven

MARTY'S REMARK hung in the air for a moment. Nancy and Ned exchanged a look of shock.

"Are you accusing Jane of—" Ned began.

"Whoa," Marty said, holding up a hand, palm out. "I'm not accusing anyone. But think about it. Here's Jane, desperate to stay in business. Ursula, who is worth a lot of money to her, says she's leaving. It's too much for Jane, who blows her top, and Ursula winds up dead. It's a possibility, that's all I'm saying."

He was saying a lot, Nancy thought. He had made Jane a strong suspect in Ursula's death.

Marty stood up and smiled, switching back to the smooth, fast-talking agent. "Ned, I don't want to pressure you," he said. "But think about signing a letter saying that you'll join us when your deal with JZA expires. That way, your future is protected when—*if* JZA goes belly up. I'd hate to see a promising career like yours flame out before it gets off the ground. Oh, speaking of getting off the ground, have fun tomorrow. Hot-air balloon rides can be very exciting."

Ned and Nancy exchanged a look, and Ned muttered, "I'll give it some thought."

But as they left the office, Nancy knew Ned was thinking the same thing she was: How did Marty know about the balloon?

Nancy was lost in thought as Ned drove them back to JZA. Their route took them through the business district, but Nancy hardly noticed the huge buildings towering on either side.

Apparently she had been too ready to assume Marty's guilt. Could he be just what he claimed to be, a hustler whose drive and ambition had forced Jane to the wall? If so, why had Ursula saved the threatening notes along with Marty's innocent ones behind her mirror? Or had someone else put them there? In any event, there were questions for Jane to answer, and soon.

Ned turned to Nancy while they waited at a traffic light. "Marty makes a good case for himself. If I was really thinking seriously about a career as an actor, I'd consider his offer."

Nancy swung around to face Ned. *"Are* you thinking seriously about acting?"

"I'm going back to Emerson to finish my degree," he said. "But I might take an acting course next year. Emerson has a good drama department. It's always smart to keep your options open."

"So you are thinking about it," Nancy said.

Ned nodded emphatically. "Sure!" he exclaimed. "All of a sudden people are telling me I could make a ton of money, be a star, all that stuff. Of course I'm giving it some thought. Why does it bother you so much?"

"I don't know," Nancy said, avoiding eye contact. How could she tell him that she saw their lives spinning off in opposite directions? That she'd hoped this vacation would bring them closer together, not farther apart?

The rest of the drive went by in silence.

They walked into JZA to find that much had been accomplished in less than a day. The front room was clear of debris, though still unusable. A small back office had been made into a temporary reception room, drab and bare. Holly sat at a small desk, looking unsettled and out of place.

"Is Jane free?" Nancy asked.

Holly wheeled her chair over so that she could see into Jane's office. "It looks that way," she said, adding, "The intercom is out. We're operating with the bare necessities."

Nancy and Ned found Jane and Evan hunched over a table covered with papers. Open cartons were stacked throughout the cramped space.

"Hi," Jane said. "Like our new look?"

"Casual—yet cluttered," Ned teased. "Nice."

"Well, it's just temporary," Nancy replied.

"The place will be as good as new in a day or so. Make yourselves comfortable," Evan said, pointing to some folding chairs by the wall.

Nancy told them about Marty's note to Ned and their visit to Top Flight.

Jane scowled. "I have to admit it, Marty doesn't let grass grow under his feet. What was your impression?" she asked.

"He's smooth, and he didn't make overt threats," Nancy said. "But he implied them. There are a couple of things we should discuss."

"Such as?" Jane asked.

"First of all, we saw Tina coming out of Top Flight as we arrived," Nancy reported.

Jane shrugged. "What of it?"

"Isn't she a client of yours?" Ned asked.

"As I said before, she's registered here," Jane said. "She's free to register with other agents, as long as she isn't under contract."

"I see," Nancy said. "She also said Marty was angry with her for telling the police about him. He hinted that she'd be sorry."

"That sounds like Marty, all right," Jane commented dryly.

"The other thing," Nancy went on, "is that Marty claims Ursula Biemann had decided to leave you and sign with Top Flight."

Jane and Evan gaped at Nancy. "That's ridiculous," Jane said.

"You weren't aware of her plans?" Ned asked.

"There were no such plans," Jane insisted. "Ursula knew we were doing a good job for her."

"The thing is," Nancy continued, "Marty has a letter of intent, signed by Ursula, saying she was switching."

Evan's mouth dropped open in astonishment. "You saw this note?" he asked.

Ned nodded. "He said her death hurt Top Flight, since she was going over to them."

Jane shook her head. "That letter is a fake."

"A forgery?" Nancy shrugged. "It could be. But was it possible for Ursula to make the switch? When was her contract with JZA due to expire?"

"At the end of the month," Jane replied. "But she had no reason to leave JZA."

The room was completely silent.

"You don't believe me?" Jane's eyes flashed. "You take Marty's word over mine? Whose business was torched? Whose card was in Ursula's purse?"

"We don't know how Marty's card got there. And speaking of the fire—" Nancy was interrupted by Holly, who stood in the doorway.

"Lieutenant Antonio and Inspector Matsuda are here to see you," she said.

Jane sighed, tossing aside a photo. "I can see we won't get much work done today. Send them in, Holly."

The tall, thin lieutenant and the fire inspector

strode through the door as Evan set up two more folding chairs.

Ned stood up. "We'd better go."

"Stick around if you like," Antonio said. "Ms. Drew is working for you, Ms. Zachary?"

"Yes." Jane frowned. "At least, I hope so."

"I am," Nancy answered.

Antonio nodded. "I called River Heights yesterday," he explained. "They say that you don't get in their way and that you've actually been of help now and then. I stand corrected."

Nancy smiled. "No harm done."

"Nasty business here last night," said the lieutenant. "Good thing it wasn't worse."

"It's bad enough," Jane replied.

"Inspector Matsuda and I think there might be a connection between the fire and the death of Ursula Biemann," Antonio announced.

"The fire was definitely arson," the inspector said. "Funny thing, though. Whoever did it cut power to your alarm and sprinkler systems, which implies knowledge and experience. But the fire was started by gasoline-soaked rags, which are easily detected. No pro would do that—unless they wanted it to look like arson."

"But why?" Ned asked, looking mystified.

Lieutenant Antonio fixed Jane with an intent look. "We understand your insurance on this place comes to quite a bit more than the offices and furnishings are worth. Why?" he asked.

"Because we're more than just offices and furnishings," Jane said.

Seeing the beleaguered look on Jane's face, Nancy found herself feeling sorry for the agent, despite her own suspicions.

"Not everything can be put into ledgers," Jane explained. "Our files, photos, contact lists, demo tapes—if we'd lost all of them, we would have had to shut down for a while. Many of our clients would have looked elsewhere for representation, and we'd probably have been finished. What's your point?"

"Motive is our point, Ms. Zachary," said the inspector. Nancy thought his style was gentler than the lieutenant's, but he was just as tough underneath. "That fire was meant to destroy this place, and it was set up to look like arson. Did you start the fire as a way to get out of a bad hole by collecting the insurance money?"

"*And* cast suspicion on your biggest rival, Marty Prince?" the policeman added. "I hear Top Flight Artists had persuaded Ursula Biemann to sign with them just before she died. I can see why you might want to get Prince out of your way."

"I think you've been misinformed about Ursula's plans." Jane looked from one man to the other, and Nancy saw that her hands were clenched.

Nancy had an idea that put Jane in a somewhat

less sinister light. "There's another way to look at the fire," she said. "Maybe someone wanted the arson to look obvious so it would be hard for Jane to get compensation. As long as she's a suspect, the insurance company won't pay a cent, right?"

"You have a point," admitted the inspector.

Jane gave Nancy a brief smile. Then, with icy politeness, she turned back to the men. "Other than telling me I'm a suspect, is there anything else? I still have a business to run."

"Not right now," Lieutenant Antonio said. "We know where to find you if need be." He turned to Nancy. "Let me know if you learn anything."

"Of course," Nancy replied.

The two men got up and walked out.

Jane breathed deeply. "Thanks for bailing me out," she said to Nancy.

"I'm on your side," Nancy assured her.

Just then Holly stuck her head through the door. "Message for Ned from Freddy Estevez."

Ned took the note, read it, and groaned. "I report for work tomorrow morning at six."

Evan laughed. "Welcome to the wonderful world of show business."

"Ned—" Nancy paused with her chopsticks in midair—"have you heard a word I said?"

Ned swallowed a mouthful of fried rice, his

eyes darting over to Nancy. "Sure, Nan. I'm just kind of tired of talking about the case—and a little nervous about the commercial tomorrow."

Since Ned had to be up at the crack of dawn, Jane had suggested that he and Nancy catch an early dinner in Chinatown, a famous village of tiny restaurants and apartments crowded into a few hilly blocks.

When Ned and Nancy had walked under a huge red archway that marked off the neighborhood, Nancy had thought that colorful Chinatown would be the perfect place to talk things out. But once they were settled at a table with an array of rice, dumplings, stir-fried vegetables, and shrimp before them, Nancy could see that Ned was a thousand miles away. Instead of talking, they concentrated on eating.

"I'd better call it a night," Ned said, yawning as their plates were cleared away.

Wrapped in their own thoughts, they walked to their rental car.

When Ned and Nancy arrived at the Chandlers', Nancy decided to call Lieutenant Antonio to see if he had learned any additional information about the case.

"Any news on Ursula's killing?" Nancy asked when the lieutenant was on the line.

"I've got some background on Sean McKearn," Antonio said. "Two arrests for assault and battery. The first time the victim wouldn't testify against him. The second time McKearn got probation. He's a wrong number for sure."

"Did the mallet in Ursula's wastebasket belong to him?" Nancy asked. "It had his initial, and it might be something a sculptor would use."

"It was Sean's," the lieutenant said. "He uses it to drive a chisel into wood. He says he doesn't know how it got to Ursula's place. The stain on the mallet was blood, but we haven't identified the type yet. Sean is a prime suspect. But there are still many unanswered questions."

"Did you find the typewriter that was used to write the notes to Ursula?" Nancy asked.

"No luck," said the lieutenant. "None of the typewriters at Top Flight matched."

"Any other news?" Nancy asked.

"Her death was caused by a blow from a blunt instrument, probably that mallet. It happened between nine in the evening and six o'clock the morning you found her. Also, we're pretty sure she wasn't killed in that alley."

Nancy nodded. "The scuff marks on the backs of her shoes suggest she was dragged, right?"

Antonio chuckled. "Right you are."

"I think it's more likely she was killed the evening before we found her rather than that morning," Nancy said.

"How do you figure that?" the lieutenant asked.

"Her clothes," Nancy replied. "She was dressed for a night out. Not even an actress would wear an off-the-shoulder gown to work."

Lieutenant Antonio sounded impressed. "That's a good observation, Nancy. I'll keep it in mind."

Nancy told the lieutenant she'd keep in touch and hung up.

Checking her watch, Nancy said to Ned, "I'm going to take a quick walk around the block. It's still early."

"I'd join you, but I'm totally wiped out," he said. "You sure you'll be okay?"

"I'll be fine," she assured him.

Ned shrugged, then nodded. "Okay, Nan. See you in the morning." He went upstairs.

He didn't even kiss me good night, Nancy thought, her heart aching as she walked down the quiet, tree-lined street.

The Chandlers lived a block from the edge of the bay, near the marina yacht basin. Nancy headed that way, noticing how the fog made the headlights of passing cars look ghostly. If there were other pedestrians around, she couldn't see them. It was as if the mist had wrapped her up in a private world.

Lost in thought, she walked slowly toward the bay. The damp air chilled her and began to soak her jacket, but she hardly noticed. She was as far from solving her case as when she had started.

Things were still not right between her and Ned, and she didn't know how to deal with it.

At the water's edge, waves lapped the shore and boats rocked at anchor. A foghorn echoed out in the bay. Surely she and Ned would—

Footsteps sounded in the fog, from somewhere nearby. Nancy looked around, but the mist was too thick and she couldn't see a thing.

As she peered around, the footsteps stopped. A man's voice chuckled, just loud enough to be heard. It was a nasty, menacing sound.

"Who's there?" Nancy called out.

"Just me," the voice said. She still couldn't see the speaker, but she heard footsteps approaching. Icy panic shot through her.

"You know what curiosity did to the cat?" the voice growled. Nancy swung around to her left. A hulking shape loomed.

Sean McKearn stood a few feet from her, an ugly smirk on his face. "Surprise," he murmured.

How did he know where to find me? Nancy thought frantically. What does he want? She looked around, trying to decide how to escape. This guy was huge and extremely dangerous.

Swiftly, his right hand shot out, and Nancy's arm was clamped tight.

Sean brought his face to within inches of hers. His eyes were wide and fiery.

"You're messing with the wrong dude," he growled. "Now I'm going to teach you a lesson."

101

Chapter

Twelve

NANCY SQUIRMED, trying to break free. But Sean had an iron grip, and she couldn't slip away.

There were no other people in sight, and Nancy knew that passing motorists wouldn't be able to see them in the mist. But if she could just break loose and scramble away, she had a chance of losing him in the dense fog.

"What are you trying to do to me?" snarled Sean, shaking Nancy.

"Do to you?" Nancy repeated, puzzled as well as scared. "I didn't do anything."

Sean pulled her close enough so that she could feel his breath on her face. A muscle twitched in his cheek. "I heard otherwise!" he barked. "How did you get it out of my studio?"

Now Nancy was totally confused. "Get what?"

"'Get what?'" he mimicked. "My hammer,

that's what—as if you didn't know. I should've worked it out myself. I catch you poking around Ursula's place, and then the cops find my hammer in her garbage. They say it's the murder weapon. You planted it! Who are you working for?"

Through a haze of pain, a phrase Sean had used echoed in her mind: I heard otherwise. "Sean, did someone say I set you up? If they did, they were lying! They're using you to get at me!"

It made sense; someone was using Sean as a weapon against her.

"I'm tired of playing games," he said, grabbing her coat collar with his left hand. His right hand still held her forearm like a steel band. "Tell me who put you up to it!"

"No one!" Nancy insisted, writhing. Her jacket collar slipped out of his hand, and in a flash Nancy realized that the damp cloth was slippery.

Summoning all her concentration, she wheeled back, jerking her body away from him. Although she couldn't break free, she felt Sean's hand slip along the sleeve of her jacket.

The instant his grip relaxed, Nancy pulled away, but Sean came lunging toward her.

Leaping back, she had no time to think before she landed a karate kick to Sean's chest. The blow shocked him momentarily, giving her a chance to escape.

She dodged to her right and began to run, knowing that safety was only a block away.

Bellowing, he hurled himself at her, hands outstretched. She felt one hand close around her ankle, then slip away. The jolt made Nancy stumble forward, and she felt her head graze the pavement as she landed.

Don't stop now, she told herself. Within seconds, she was back on her feet, racing off. As she ran, she looked back over her shoulder, but could see only the fog.

His hoarse voice rang out from the mist, "We aren't done yet! I'll get you!"

Panting, Nancy reached the Chandlers' door and pounded on it.

Laurel opened the door and gasped. "Nancy! There's blood on your face! What happened?"

In a hall mirror, Nancy saw a trickle of red on her forehead. It was a small cut—minor compared to what could have happened. "I must have scraped it when I fell on the ground," she said as Laurel motioned her into the kitchen.

"Sean McKearn found me," Nancy added, sagging into a chair. "He thinks I'm trying to frame him for murder. I managed to get away."

"Why does he think that?" Laurel asked.

Nancy suddenly felt very drained. "Somebody must have planted the idea in his mind."

"Let me get the first-aid kit," Laurel said.

While she was gone, Nancy considered Sean. Did this mean that he was innocent? Not necessarily, she decided, not with his temper.

Laurel came in and cleaned and bandaged the slight cut. "Evan's still at work," she said. "What are you going to do? You're in danger!"

"I must be getting close to some answers, though I still don't see what they are."

"Oh, I almost forgot," Laurel said. "Someone from the production office called for you and Ned early this evening. Evan had told me you were going to Chinatown, so I passed it on. Did the caller find you?"

Nancy sat up straight. "Who was it?"

Laurel shrugged.

"Was it a man or a woman?" Nancy asked.

Laurel paused, thinking, and laughed. "It's funny, but now that you ask, I'm not sure. The voice was strange. It sounded like the caller had laryngitis or something. Does it matter?"

Nancy realized that the caller might have been Sean, trying to locate her. Maybe he followed us from the restaurant, Nancy thought. But she saw no reason to upset Laurel by telling her.

"No, it doesn't matter," she said. "I'm going to turn in. It's been a long day, and I want to see Ned before he leaves in the morning."

Nancy slept poorly and woke up while it was still dark. The illuminated dial of her clock read five o'clock. She heard voices downstairs—Ned and Evan. She pulled on jeans, a sweater, and running shoes and went down.

Evan looked up from the kitchen table and put a finger to his lips. "Shh," he whispered. "We're letting Laurel sleep in."

Nancy thought that Evan could have used several hours of sleep himself. His eyes were red-rimmed and had dark circles underneath them.

"Why are you up so early?" Nancy asked Evan.

"I'm going out to the location," Evan explained. "Jane was supposed to go, but with the fire damage she wants to stay at the agency."

"Mind if I come along?" Nancy asked.

"No problem," Evan said.

"Is it all right with you, Ned?" she asked.

Although Ned didn't seem thrilled by the idea, he shrugged and said, "Why not?" Glancing over at Nancy, his eyes narrowed and he reached out to touch her forehead. "What happened to you?"

Nancy frowned. "I ran into Sean McKearn last night." With worried looks, Ned and Evan heard her story.

"I feel awful about having gotten you mixed up in this," Evan said.

"Don't feel bad," she assured him. "It's part of what I do. I've learned to live with it."

"I should have been there!" Ned insisted.

"Don't blame yourself," Nancy urged. "There was no reason to expect it to happen."

Sensing that the couple needed privacy, Evan headed out to the garage, saying, "I'll warm up the car."

Looking at Nancy, Ned shook his head, obviously upset. "You say you're worried about being closed out of my life," he told her. "How do you think I feel when you're wrapped up in a case and I'm closed out? I worry about you. I care about you, Nan."

Surprised by Ned's words, Nancy reached out and squeezed his hand. "I care about you, too," she said. "We'll work this out, I know we will."

In the sparse predawn traffic, the drive to the production company took only fifteen minutes. It was still dark when Evan parked. Two minivans were waiting, their motors idling.

Freddy got out of one and walked over to them. "Good morning. We're almost ready to go."

"I'm going to take Jane's place at the shoot, if that's all right," Evan said.

"Sure," Freddy said. "But Ned should go in the van, so we can go over the plans for the day."

"Okay," Ned said, getting out of the car. On the drive over, Ned had been preoccupied and silent. Now he turned to Nancy with a troubled expression and seemed about to say something. But he only sighed and said, "See you later."

Nancy watched him walk away. As he got in the van, she heard Amanda call out, "Hey, Tex!"

The sun was coming up as Evan crossed the Golden Gate Bridge. They drove through Marin County and then headed east.

Nancy looked at Evan. "Don't answer this question if it puts you in an awkward position."

The agent gave her a sidelong, troubled glance. "Do you suspect Jane of something?"

"You'll keep what I say in confidence?"

"Sure," he said. "But I can't believe she'd do anything illegal. And Jane would never damage her agency. It's been her life's work."

"I know JZA is important to her," Nancy said. "Would it be important enough for her to use desperate measures to save it from shutting down?"

"I don't know," Evan said, shaking his head. "I can't believe Jane would stoop so low."

Deciding to let the subject drop, Nancy watched the scenery for the rest of the trip.

At eight o'clock they swung into a clearing off the road. "We're here," Evan said after the hour-long drive through vineyards and farms. The field was cluttered with vehicles, including a big tractor-trailer and a few smaller trucks. Cables, lights, and reflectors were being unloaded.

Nancy got out, stretched, and looked around. They were in a meadow between rugged hills and rock formations. A helicopter sat in the grass, and farther from the road a huge expanse of gold and red nylon was spread on the ground—the balloon. Next to it was a giant wicker basket.

Curious, Nancy walked over to look. Two big electric fans blew air into the mouth of the balloon. The top was already billowing sluggishly as it inflated. Two men hauled a piece of machinery into place at the balloon's mouth. Nancy noticed a cylindrical fuel tank attached to the mechanism. The men adjusted its position, and one man gave a thumbs-up sign.

"Better stand back," said a voice nearby.

Nancy turned to see a tall, athletic-looking blond woman next to her. Nancy stepped away from the balloon just as a long blue jet of flame roared out of the fuel tank.

"You came with Evan Chandler, right?" the blonde asked. When Nancy introduced herself, the woman shook her hand. "I'm Peg Amarillo, with the ground crew. Ever see a balloon close up?"

Nancy shook her head, fascinated.

Peg pointed to the flame. "The burner is fastened under the mouth of the balloon, in the basket, which we call the gondola. It heats the air inside, and when the air is hot enough, up you go. If you want to go higher, a blast from the burner heats the air some more. If you want to go down, you let hot air out of a vent in the side by pulling a cord attached to the gondola, where the passengers ride. Simple."

"How do you turn?" Nancy asked.

"You can't," Peg replied, grinning. "You go where the winds blow. If you don't like where you're going, you try to catch a breeze in another direction by going up or down. To get down real fast, there's a rip panel in the top, fastened with Velcro. Yank that off and you'll come down."

"Peg!" called one of the men working the burner. "Give us a hand here, will you?"

"Sorry, duty calls," Peg said, hurrying away.

Nancy saw that breakfast had been laid out on a table. She picked up an orange and spotted Ned coming out of a trailer, where he had changed into his dude ranch outfit. Resisting an impulse to giggle, she grabbed another orange and joined him.

"Care for some breakfast, cowboy?" she asked.

"Thanks." He looked down at his costume and scowled. "If any of the guys from my frat see me in this stupid getup, I'll never live it down."

Nancy wanted to clear the air with Ned and hoped they had a few free minutes. "What were you trying to tell me before?"

Ned looked deep into her eyes. "I—"

"Ah, there you are!" A tall gangly man in a khaki fatigue jacket and bush hat appeared. Amanda walked beside him. "I'm Keith Bryant," he said, extending his hand. "I'm directing this masterpiece. Nice meeting you, Ned."

"Same here." Ned shook the offered hand. "Meet Nancy Drew, my girlfriend."

"Pleasure," Keith said, smiling at Nancy. "We'll do the balloon stuff first because the wind is right. Later we'll shoot you picnicking in the meadow, drinking King Kola, naturally. For the balloon shots, the camera will be in a helicopter. I'll coordinate it from the ground by radio. All you have to do is smile and wave and look like you're having a blast. Any questions?"

"Sounds easy," Ned remarked.

"You'll get your shots in a flash," Amanda promised. "Ned and I have an amazing chemistry."

"Okay," Keith said. "Enjoy the ride, and we'll do the work."

A woman with a clipboard ran up to them. "We're all set, Keith."

Keith nodded. "Fantastic! Let's do it."

They walked over to the balloon, which was now fully inflated, held down with ropes by the ground crew. It looked like a forty-foot-high red and gold teardrop. The pilot stood in the gondola. Ned climbed aboard and helped Amanda in.

"Cast off!" the pilot called, and the ground crew let go of the ropes. The balloon rose slowly. Ned and Amanda waved to the people below.

Evan came up beside Nancy. "Some fun, huh?"

She nodded, watching it float upward.

By the time the helicopter took off, the balloon was about two hundred feet high.

"Ned? Amanda? How are you doing?" Keith called into the radio.

Ned's voice crackled through the receiver. "This is awesome! The view is great, and there's no noise. Everything is smooth as silk."

"Okay, stand by." Keith looked up, shading his eyes with his hand. Then he called the camera operator in the helicopter. "Get that sheer rock wall to the east in your shot, okay?"

"Can do," came the reply.

"Hold on," said a voice over the radio, and Nancy realized it was the balloon pilot. "We've got a little problem."

Nancy looked up. The balloon was drifting toward the hills, and its gondola was swaying.

"Hang on tight, you two!" the pilot called. "We have a strong wind here that's taking us toward the hills too fast. We have to gain altitude and find a gentler breeze."

"Roger," Keith replied, looking up anxiously.

The balloon was now too far away for Nancy to make out the passengers.

The pilot came on the radio, obvious tension in his voice. "Something's wrong with the burner! It's flamed out, and it won't relight! We can't get away from this wind! If we hit that bluff, it'll collapse the balloon or tip the gondola!"

Far above, the balloon rolled violently. On the radio, Nancy heard a scream of terror from Amanda as the gondola rocked back and forth.

"Easy, I've got you!" Ned's voice said. Nancy stared up, feeling helpless and horrified.

The balloon was completely at the mercy of a powerful wind, and it was being blown right into a sheer escarpment of jagged rocks!

Chapter

Thirteen

PEG SPOKE into her radio. "How about venting air and going lower?"

"Too slow," the pilot replied. "We'll hit the rocks too soon."

"Then pull the rip panel!" Peg shouted.

"No way," the pilot's voice crackled over the radio. "The terrain is too rocky for a safe hard landing. You'd better come and get us."

"Hang on—we're coming!" Peg and two other crew members sprinted toward an all-terrain vehicle parked by the road.

Nancy dashed along with them. "What will you do?" she asked Peg.

"He'll drop lines over the side, and we'll grab on and pull them out of danger." Peg and the others scrambled into the ATV. "Come on!" she urged Nancy. "We can use another hand."

Nancy jumped in, and the ATV roared to life and jolted toward the hills. As they bounced along, she clung to the door handle and focused on the balloon overhead. It had lost height but was closer to the jagged outcroppings.

As Nancy watched, the gondola rocked, and Amanda's scream was heard on Peg's radio. A tiny figure was almost tossed over the side. It was Ned! Nancy held her breath as he caught hold of the rigging and hauled himself back in.

The ground got steeper and rougher, but the ATV was closing in on the balloon. Suddenly they were at the foot of a slope too rugged even for a four-wheel-drive. Peg grabbed the radio.

"We're close!" she called. "Drop the lines!"

Two ropes snaked out of the gondola and dropped to earth. Nancy and the crew scrambled upward on treacherous footing. One rope had landed just yards from Nancy. She was heading toward it when some loose rock gave way under her and she fell. She got up, ignoring the pain of a bruised knee, but she had lost sight of the rope!

She was flat against a rock face, feet braced on a ledge. To her left, Peg shouted. She turned and noted with dismay that the others were still far from the other line. Nancy looked up and saw the balloon ominously close to a sharp stone spur. Her eyes followed the rope down from the gondola, and she saw that it was snagged in a bush twenty feet away.

She crawled forward, clinging to every tiny crevice. The distance to the line narrowed. At length, gauging the distance, she took a deep breath and lunged to the side, her right arm outstretched. Her hand closed around the rope!

"I've got it!" she shouted, getting a firmer grip with both hands. Wrapping it around her waist, she pulled in the slack and slid down to a more level surface. The rope kept pulling at her as though it were alive and had a mind to escape.

The crew called out encouragement and hurried over to her. By the time they reached her, Nancy's arms ached from her effort. Together the four tugged the line downward, muscling it back to the ATV. They tied the rope to the vehicle's roll bar and put it into reverse.

Nancy kept her eyes skyward, afraid to breathe as long as Ned remained in danger. It seemed to take forever, but finally the balloon was pulled away from the escarpment, toward safer ground and a soft landing.

The pilot's voice came on over the radio. "Well done! I'm bringing us down."

Nancy felt relief wash over her as the balloon drifted to earth. Two minutes later the gondola thumped down and tilted over, as the balloon crumpled in a mass of gold and red nylon.

Ned stumbled from the gondola with Amanda clinging to him. Nancy dashed forward.

Seeing Nancy running toward him, Ned gently

freed himself from Amanda's grip and ran to meet her. Nancy let out a cry as he wrapped his arms around her. Breathless, they hugged each other.

"I was so afraid," she murmured, her face buried against his chest. "I thought . . . you almost . . ." She couldn't say the words.

Gently Ned touched Nancy's chin and lifted her face. They kissed, and a rush of emotion surged through Nancy. The touch of Ned's lips filled her with the knowledge that everything would be all right between them. The near miss had proven just how much she loved Ned.

"For a minute I thought I was a goner," he said softly. "That's when I realized how much you mean to me. Nothing matters to me as much as you do. I must have been a little crazy lately to lose sight of that. I almost lost you."

"Don't think about it now," Nancy whispered happily. "You're alive and well and with me, and that's all that counts."

There was a sudden outburst of angry voices behind them. Evan was shouting at Freddy, who looked gray and drawn. Nancy took Ned's arm as the two men approached.

"It was crazy, this balloon idea," Evan yelled. "I should never have allowed my clients to risk their necks in that contraption."

The balloon pilot, who had been poking through his gear, spun around. "Balloons are perfectly safe!" he insisted. "I've gone up thousands of times, and nothing like this ever happened before."

"What went wrong this time?" Keith asked.

"I'm trying to figure that out right now," said the pilot, bending over the burner.

Freddy Estevez bit his lip and checked his watch. "Thank heavens everyone is all right," he said. "Well, what should we do now?"

Evan stared at him, astonished. "What we should do—no, what we *will* do—is pack it in for today. Nobody here is ready to go back to work. We'll reschedule and be thankful we got away with nothing more than a narrow escape."

"But—" Freddy looked at the grim faces around him. "Of course you're right. We'll reschedule. We'll call it off for today."

Keith excused himself and left to supervise.

Amanda approached Ned and Nancy. She was pale and shaken. "I've never been so frightened in my life."

"It was scary," Ned agreed, his arm around Nancy. "But the main thing is, nobody was hurt."

Amanda looked wistfully at Ned, then nodded. "Thank goodness," she said. She caught Nancy's eye and smiled, as if to say "no hard feelings." Nancy smiled back, too happy to carry a grudge. Amanda slowly walked back toward the trailers.

"Hey!" The pilot held up a small piece of machinery. "Here's what caused our problem. This feed valve connects the fuel line to the burner. It was stuck in an open position, and all our butane leaked out. That's why I couldn't relight the burner—there was nothing to burn."

Nancy walked over and examined the valve. "You mean it was defective?" she asked.

"No way!" the pilot insisted. "I do a thorough preflight check every time I go up, and I mean *thorough*. I check everything: fabric, vent, rip panel, rigging, the burner and fuel supply—the works. After all, *my* life depends on this equipment, too. There was nothing defective on this balloon before we went up."

"When did you do the check?" Nancy asked.

"We started at six-thirty this morning, and finished about an hour later. We did the same careful job we always do," the pilot said firmly, as if daring anyone to contradict him.

"No one is blaming you for what happened today," Evan said.

Production crew members started packing their trucks while the balloon crew set about carefully folding the huge expanse of nylon fabric and detaching the rigging.

Nancy and Ned remained in a huddle with Evan and the pilot. Ned rubbed his jaw, looking perplexed. "So why did the valve malfunction?"

"Maybe it was metal fatigue," Evan said. "After a while, things just wear out."

"No, sir," the pilot insisted. "I always replace equipment long before it can wear out. That valve is almost brand-new."

"May I take it?" Nancy asked. "I'd like to have it examined."

"What are you talking about?" demanded the pilot. "I just *did* examine it, I told you!"

"I mean for fingerprints," Nancy explained.

The pilot stared at her. "Who would do something like that deliberately?"

"It's just a precaution." Nancy preferred to avoid a detailed explanation of her suspicions.

The pilot frowned but handed over the valve, which Nancy placed in a tissue. "I don't know what to make of this, but go ahead," he said. "I want to know how this happened as much as anybody else. More, even." He left to help his crew pack up.

"Nancy, was this sabotage?" Evan stared at her and lowered his voice, making sure that no one was within earshot. "Does it tie in with Ursula's death?"

"It would be pretty wild if it wasn't related somehow," Nancy said.

Ned's jaw was clenched. "I want to find out who rigged this. Three of us almost died!"

"For what it's worth," Nancy said, "I don't think the culprit meant to kill anyone, just force the balloon to land prematurely and stop the shooting. No one could count on the wind almost blowing you into the rocks."

Ned still looked grim. "Even if the person didn't mean it, we could have been killed."

"I have questions to ask while everyone is still

here," Nancy said. Looking around, she saw the balloon pilot and his crew loading gear into a truck. She went over with Ned and Evan.

"Did you notice any strangers today who didn't have legitimate business here?" Nancy asked. "Anyone hanging around your stuff?"

"I used my regular people," the pilot replied. "But the commercial guys are new to me. Some of them watched us, but I didn't see anything unusual."

Nancy thanked him and headed over to Keith. She asked him the same questions.

"There are always rubberneckers," said the director, thinking back. "Mostly they're locals. Shooting commercials fascinates people and they love to gawk. I didn't know the balloon crew. I can't say I saw anything odd. But I was busy, so I wasn't observant." He looked toward his crew. "Tammy! Got a minute?"

The young woman with the clipboard came up.

"Did you see anyone suspicious today?" he asked. "Snooping around the balloon?"

"Just a few bystanders, as usual," she said. "There are always new faces. But guess what? I was putting papers in the van and found this on the driver's seat. Is it supposed to be a joke?"

She gave Keith a sheet of notepaper. He read it and frowned, adding, "It's a lousy joke, if you ask me."

He handed the paper to Evan and walked

angrily away. Evan opened it, holding it for Nancy and Ned to read as he did.

The note had been handprinted in block lettering: Avoid expensive delays and get the best results. Use Top Flight actors.

Nancy had seen the gray parchment paper before. She could almost guess what would be printed at the top before she saw it: From the desk of Marty Prince.

Chapter

Fourteen

"MARTY PRINCE!" Ned exclaimed. "I should've known."

"Don't jump to conclusions," Nancy cautioned him. "The note is unsigned, and just because it's on his letterhead—"

"'Hot-air balloon rides can be very exciting!'" Ned quoted. "That's what he told us."

"You've lost me," Evan confessed.

"Remember, Nan?" Ned's voice had an undercurrent of anger. "It was the last thing Marty said to us yesterday. Oh, it was exciting, all right! When we get back to San Francisco, I'll show him how exciting it was."

"Marty said that to you yesterday?" Evan asked. "But that means—"

"It means he knew Ned was doing a commercial with a balloon sequence," Nancy said. "We don't know that it means anything else, for sure."

"You don't understand," Evan protested. "My question is, how did he find out about Ned getting the job so quickly? He left a note for you at the house early yesterday morning, and you had only signed the contract the previous day."

"I asked him that, as a matter of fact," Ned replied. "He said something about news traveling fast in the small world of talent agencies."

"Maybe," Evan allowed, "but not that fast."

Nancy nodded. "I see what you mean. It sounds as if someone connected with JZA has been slipping information to Marty secretly."

"Doesn't the fact that Top Flight's name keeps coming up in situations like this tell you something?" Ned asked.

"Yes," Nancy replied, "but not what you think it does. The first time I heard of Top Flight Artists was when we found Ursula's body. There was a Top Flight card in her purse, where no one could possibly miss it. It struck me as odd. I mean, if Marty had killed Ursula, or hired someone to do it, he'd be sure to remove anything that connected him to her, right?

"There are also the notes in Ursula's apartment," Nancy added. "Marty's notes were tucked in with the anonymous threats."

"Which signifies what?" Evan asked.

"Marty's name keeps popping up in all the

wrong places," Nancy explained. "Evan, you say Marty's clever. Does a clever man leave such obvious clues to implicate himself in serious crimes?"

"I suppose not," Evan admitted. "Is someone trying to set him up for things he didn't do?"

"That's my guess," Nancy answered, hooking an arm through Ned's. "This doesn't mean Marty's completely innocent, only that he may not be quite as bad as he's been made to look."

"Who's doing it?" Ned asked.

Nancy thought back to what she had heard at JZA over the last few days. "I'm not sure yet. When can we head back to San Francisco?"

"Let's go now," Evan offered.

As they walked back to the car, Nancy turned to Ned. "You can have the backseat all to yourself. Maybe you can get a little sleep."

"Sleep?" Ned snorted. "My nerves are still standing on end. I won't be able to sleep for a month."

Evan's car topped a hill and San Francisco Bay suddenly appeared, along with the Golden Gate Bridge. Ned was in the backseat and Nancy was next to Evan. She had been quiet, thinking about the case. Obviously, someone was trying to implicate Marty Prince. Also, someone at Jane Zachary Associates had been passing Marty information to use against JZA. It appeared that someone was trying to help Marty while someone else was framing him. The two things seemed to work at cross-purposes. Something didn't add up.

Ned leaned forward and put a hand on Nancy's shoulder. "What about Sean?" he asked. "Did he attack you last night just to scare you off the case? Or was he trying to get rid of you before you nail him for murder?"

She put her hand over his. "If Sean's mallet turns out to be the murder weapon, the odds of him being guilty go down," Nancy said. "If he *did* use the mallet to kill Ursula, why would he drop it in her apartment?" She shook her head. "I think it was planted there to implicate him."

"Just as Marty's notes were planted to implicate him," Ned said.

"Right," Nancy said. "And the bottom line is that I have to find out who at JZA is helping Marty Prince. That's my job, remember? I'd also like to know how Sean knew where to find me."

"Can I drop you anywhere before I go back to the agency?" Evan asked.

"We'll go with you to JZA," Nancy said.

They drove past the Presidio army base and Golden Gate Park. By the time they arrived at the agency, it was afternoon.

When they stepped into JZA's main office, Tina Grayce emerged from a work station with an armload of papers. She seemed surprised to see them. "Weren't you up in Napa doing that balloon thing today?" she asked.

"We had a little accident," Ned said.

"'Little accident' nothing!" Evan insisted. "Ned's lucky to be alive!"

Tina's delicate features hardened in shock. "That . . . that's awful," she said. "How did—"

"We were almost blown into some rocks by a gale," Ned explained. "We couldn't get out of the wind because— Whoops, take it easy."

Tina's papers cascaded to the floor as she gaped at Ned. "You were nearly killed?" she asked.

"It's okay," Ned assured her. "Everyone is alive and well. Can I help you with that stuff?"

Tina knelt down to gather up the mess. "No, I'll do it." Nancy watched her, noting that she seemed quite upset. "Nearly killed," she murmured, just loud enough for Nancy to hear. "What's wrong with me?"

"Let's fill Jane in," Nancy suggested.

"Good idea," Evan replied.

"She's in her office," Tina said, staring at the floor.

As Nancy, Ned, and Evan filed through her office door, Jane did a double take and put down the photo proof sheets and magnifying glass she had been working with.

"Back already?" she said. "I didn't expect to see Ned for the rest of the day."

Nancy told Jane about the balloon's near-disaster. As Jane listened, Nancy could see that she was shocked and concerned. But her gray eyes lit with anger when she heard about the note on Marty Prince's letterhead.

"What did I tell you?" the agent snapped. "Marty is nothing but a thug."

Nancy sat down across from Jane, as did Ned and Evan. "How long has Tina worked here?"

"Tina?" Jane looked puzzled, but answered, "About four months."

"Besides fixing machines, what kind of work does she do for you?" Nancy asked.

"Various odd jobs," Jane replied. Nancy saw that Ned and Evan were as curious as Jane about the point of her questions. "She does filing, answers the phones. Why?"

Nancy nodded. Another piece of the puzzle had fallen into place. "So she has access to all the addresses and phone numbers of your clients, as well as information on who's getting work."

Realization dawned on Ned. "Nan, do you think Tina is Marty's source of information?"

"It fits," Nancy said. "Remember the morning you came in to sign the contract? Jane told Tina that you had just signed, and that you'd landed the first commercial you tried out for. Tina was among the first people to know."

"That's right," Evan said, snapping his fingers. "And the next morning, Marty Prince sends Ned a note."

"Do you have a file for Ned, with our local contact information?" Nancy asked.

"Yes. When Ned signed I started a file on him,

with Evan's address and phone number in it. It was in the client files that morning." Jane looked incredulous. "But I don't understand. Why would Tina turn on me? I've been her friend, helped her, given her work . . ."

"Maybe she blames you for her lack of success," Ned suggested.

"I was always up-front with her," Jane protested. "I told her I'd do what I could for her, but that my expectations weren't high."

"But she still wants a big-time acting and modeling career," Nancy said. "I don't think she did this on her own. I bet she was working with someone who promised her what you wouldn't, who was willing to use her, even if she got hurt in the process."

Ned nodded. "I *knew* Marty was a sleaze."

"I need to call Lieutenant Antonio," Nancy said.

"Be my guest," Jane said with a smug smile. "Tell him to arrest Marty Prince."

"It's not that simple," Nancy said as she dialed. "Marty may be guilty of nothing but lying, which isn't a crime in itself. I want to exchange news with the lieutenant. . . . Yes, this is Nancy Drew for Lieutenant Antonio."

When Antonio came on the line, Nancy told him about her encounter with Sean McKearn the night before and the sabotaging of the balloon.

"Anything new on your end?" she asked.

"The blood on that mallet is definitely Ursula

Biemann's," Lieutenant Antonio said. "But the mallet's handle was wiped clean. There are no prints at all."

"So you still don't have Ursula's killer?"

"Not yet," he said. "But I have a hunch we're getting close. You watch out now."

Nancy's face was thoughtful as she hung up. "They found Ursula's blood on Sean McKearn's mallet," she told the others, "but there's no way to know who used it."

"My vote still goes to Sean himself," Ned said. "From what you say about him, I think he's just the kind of loose cannon that would bludgeon his girlfriend and not think clearly enough to hide the incriminating evidence."

Jane stood up abruptly and called her assistant in. "I *have* to ask Tina," she said. "I have to know if she's been helping Marty try to ruin JZA, and why." When Holly appeared, Jane asked, "Would you tell Tina to come in here."

"She's gone, Jane," Holly said.

"Gone?" Jane repeated. "But she said she'd be here for the rest of the day."

"When did Tina leave?" Nancy asked.

"She rushed out just after you three returned to the office," Holly said. "She seemed upset."

"Where was she going?" Jane asked.

Holly shrugged. "She didn't say." Then she added, "She did mumble something odd, though. Something about setting things right while she still has time."

"Oh, no," Nancy said, sinking back into her chair.

Ned turned to her in alarm. "Nan, are you okay? You look white as a sheet!"

She grabbed Ned's hand in her own. "We have to find Tina, right away!"

"Why?" Evan demanded. "What's the hurry?"

Nancy tightened her grip on Ned's hand as she answered, "Because she killed Ursula. And we have to act fast—or she's likely to kill someone else!"

Chapter

Fifteen

"TINA IS A MURDERER?" Jane stared at Nancy in disbelief. "That poor girl? Nancy, think again. It's hard enough to imagine Tina spying on me, but a cold-blooded killer?" She shook her head.

"I don't think she's cold-blooded at all," Nancy said. "I think she's dealing with more emotion than she can handle. She's a high-strung, nervous type. Now she's totally out of control." She stood up. "We have to find her!"

Ned was shocked by Nancy's grim expression. "What makes you say that?" he asked.

Nancy paced the room. "Did you see how she reacted when you told her about the balloon?"

"She was shocked," Ned said. "What's so strange about that? It was nearly a catastrophe."

"That's true," Nancy admitted. "But why was she shocked? I think it was guilt. The last thing I heard her say was 'What's wrong with me?' I assumed she meant that her nerves were on edge, but now I think she realized that she'd almost caused the deaths of three more people."

"You think Tina tampered with that valve?" Evan asked, raking a hand through his curly hair.

"Jane, you said Tina is good with machines— that she fixes copy machines and phones." When Jane nodded, Nancy added, "If she's that good with mechanical things, something like the valve on that fuel line would be child's play for her."

"That makes sense, I suppose," Jane said, "but she's no murderer."

"She wasn't trying to kill anyone in this case," Nancy pointed out. "All she wanted was to sabotage the commercial. Maybe she saw it as a favor to Marty. That would explain her shock at realizing that she'd almost killed a few people. What time did she get here this morning?"

Jane thought for a moment. "About ten-thirty."

Nancy made some mental calculations—and it added up. "She could have driven to Napa, sabotaged the balloon, and come back," she said. "There was plenty of time for it."

"I'd have spotted her if she'd been there," Evan protested. "So would you, for that matter."

"The pilot told us the balloon crew finished their preflight check at seven-thirty," Nancy replied. "She could have rigged the balloon and been on her way back here while we were still on the road."

"She had no business there," Ned pointed out. "Someone would have noticed her."

"The thing is," Nancy explained, "there were two groups there who didn't know each other at all—the production people and the balloon crew. Anyone seeing a stranger would have assumed that he or she was with the other crew. A few seconds to switch the valve is all she needed. If the police show Tina's photo to the crews who worked on the commercial, someone might recognize her."

"Where do you think she's going now?" Evan asked.

"If I'm right, and she realizes that she almost killed several people, I'm afraid she may want to harm herself—or maybe someone else." Nancy reached for Jane's telephone and dialed the lieutenant's number again. "Lieutenant Antonio will want to know about this," she told the group.

But the lieutenant wasn't available. Nancy was eager to share her theory, but she realized that there was no hard evidence that proved it—and it would be impossible to explain everything in a message. "Just ask him to call me here as soon as he can," Nancy said to the officer who'd answered. Then she left JZA's number.

"No luck," Nancy said as she hung up.

"What's our next step?" Ned asked.

Just then Holly appeared in the doorway, saying, "There's a call for Nancy, from Sean McKearn."

"Sean?" Nancy was astonished. "Calling me here?" She reached for Jane's phone again.

Ned's eyes narrowed suspiciously. "How did he know to call JZA?"

"Good question," Nancy said, staring at the blinking button on the phone. "For that matter, how did he know where to find me last night? I wasn't aware that he even knew my name." She punched the button. "Sean, it's Nancy Drew."

"Listen," he said in a voice so low Nancy could barely hear him, "get over to my studio right away. No tricks, no rough stuff, I promise."

"Can you speak up?" Nancy said. "I can't—"

"Tina is here. I don't want her to hear me."

"You know Tina?" Nancy asked. "Since when?"

"Look, just come, now!" Sean insisted. "She's talking about blood on her hands, wild stuff like that."

"Call the police," Nancy said emphatically.

"No!" Sean sputtered. "No cops! Cops and me don't get along. She says you're a detective. Help me handle her."

"Tina said that?" Nancy suddenly realized that there must be more history between Sean and Tina than she had realized. "Sean, there's a lot you have to tell me."

His voice became shrill with panic. "Hey,

hurry, all right? She's freaking me out. Here's my address and directions."

Nancy jotted it all down. "We're on our way."

As Nancy hung up, Ned, Evan, and Jane were staring at her expectantly. "He says Tina is there, acting crazy. He's scared," she explained. "Were you aware of any relationship between Sean and Tina?"

Jane and Evan looked at each other. Evan shook his head. "They knew each other to say hello to," Jane said. "That's all I noticed."

Nancy held up the address she'd written down. "He wants me to come to his studio as quickly as possible. Evan, can Ned and I use your car?"

"Sure," Evan said, handing her the keys. "Is there anything we can do here?"

"If the lieutenant calls, tell him that I suspect that Tina Grayce might be Ursula's killer. Tell him I think she's a threat to her own or someone else's life, and that we're on our way to find her at Sean McKearn's studio." She gave him Sean's address.

"Good luck," Jane called as Ned and Nancy left the office.

At the car, Nancy gave Ned the keys. "You drive," she said. "I'll navigate."

"Gotcha," Ned said, starting up the engine.

On the way to Sean's, Nancy sat tensely, drumming her fingers on the dashboard as Ned battled city traffic. At last, they arrived at the grimy block of lofts where Sean lived.

As they parked Ned asked, "Are Sean and Tina old friends? Why would she go to him?"

"That's something we need to find out," Nancy said as she rang the bell.

Sean opened the door. "What took you so long?" he asked. "She's gone."

"We came as fast as we could," Nancy said. "Can we come in?"

Sean's place was a spacious, high-ceilinged room, with living quarters in one corner. The rest was full of machinery, tools, and objects that Nancy decided must be pieces of sculpture—hunks of stone in odd shapes and carved wooden structures.

Thinking back to Tina's remarks about Sean's temper and personality, Nancy figured the two might have been close. She decided that a bluff was in order.

Facing Sean, she asked, "How long did you and Tina go together?"

Sean's startled reaction indicated that her bluff had worked. "How did you know we— I don't want to talk about that stuff. It's my business."

Ned stepped forward with a glint in his eyes that made Sean back away. "You're going to talk," he said, "either to us now or to the police."

Nancy spoke quickly. "When Tina said she had blood on her hands, she meant it. Let's hear about you and Tina before anyone else gets hurt."

Sean wilted. "We went together six months,

until I met Ursula. Tina was okay, she even helped out here. She's good with her hands."

"Nobody at JZA knew about you two," Ned said.

"At the time, Tina wasn't trying to make it in modeling," Sean explained. "That came later."

Things were beginning to make sense to Nancy. "So you met Ursula and dropped Tina," she prodded.

Embarrassed, Sean said, "Ursula was gorgeous and smart. And she was making tons of money."

Nancy found herself disliking Sean more and more. "When did you break up with Tina?"

"About five months ago," he answered.

Nancy nodded. "Was it after you broke up that Tina decided *she* wanted to be an actress and model and went to JZA?"

"I guess so," Sean replied. "I went to the agency one day to pick up Ursula, and there was Tina. I was afraid she might start yelling, but she just said hello and that was all there was to it. No hard feelings. Last week, she even called up and suggested that we could still be friends."

Ned turned to Nancy. "Tina must've told him about you being a detective and where we were staying," he said. "Tina was in a position to pick all that up at JZA. Right, Sean?"

"Well . . . yeah," Sean muttered.

"Was she the one who gave you the idea that I was trying to frame you?" Nancy demanded.

Sean finally met Nancy's eyes for a moment

before looking away again. "She said to watch out for you, and I knew somebody was framing me."

Nancy shook her head in exasperation. "Come on, Sean, use your head!"

"What do you mean?" he asked innocently.

"Tina's not your friend," Nancy insisted. "You dumped her. She was obsessed with losing you to Ursula. Why did she suddenly decide on a career in acting and modeling? I doubt that she cared about gaining fame and fortune. It was more like her boyfriend was stolen by a glamorous actress so she'd get back at you by becoming one, too. Or she'd get revenge on Ursula by beating her in her own field."

Nancy frowned, then continued. "But Jane couldn't give her what she needed, so she turned to Top Flight Artists, hoping to make it there. Ursula wanted to make friends with Tina, and Tina became her confidante. I think Ursula *did* decide to move to Top Flight and told Tina about her plans. To Tina, it was like saying, Now I'll be number one at Top Flight and you'll be out of luck again. That was the last straw."

Sean stared, stunned. "You mean *Tina*—"

"Yes," Nancy said grimly. "I think she worked herself up to a homicidal pitch and saw a chance to get back at Ursula and you with one move. She would kill the woman who had stolen you from her and make sure you were blamed for her murder."

Nancy walked over and pointed to a wall rack of tools. "Tina took the mallet, used it on Ursula, and left it where the police would be sure to find it, knowing they'd trace it to you, Sean."

Sean stared at Nancy as he fit the pieces of the mystery together. "What's she going to do now?" he asked.

Nancy's nerves were on edge as she turned to face Ned and Sean. "There's one other person who has treated her badly enough to be on her list of projected victims, if I'm right about what's been happening.

"That person is Marty Prince."

139

Chapter

Sixteen

W AIT A SECOND," Ned interrupted. "I thought Tina was hoping Marty could make her a success."

"Right," Nancy said. "Something must have changed. If Tina killed Ursula, she's also the one who left Marty's card in Ursula's purse. If she sabotaged the balloon, then she left that note there using Marty's personal stationery. Marty is her enemy now, and she's gone out to—how did she put it?—'set things right.'"

Confused, Ned shook his head, saying, "You have her trying to frame Sean *and* Marty for the same murder! That's not logical.'

Nancy nodded sadly. "I think Tina has gone way past logic. She's never had control of her emotions. Jane said that in auditions, she comes across as desperate. When we first met her, her nerves were stretched to the breaking point.

"Marty said that she had a habit of making ugly scenes there, and yesterday was the worst ever. Remember we met her running out of his office? She said he threatened her for talking to the police. But Marty said she begged him to sign her, and then threatened him. I think Marty's version was closer to the truth."

Nancy looked coldly at Sean. "Look at the ways she's been hurt. She lost Sean. She couldn't measure up against Ursula at JZA, or at Top Flight. Finally, something snapped. Tina couldn't handle it anymore," she finished, then asked Sean, "Where's your phone? I want to try the lieutenant again."

"On that desk," he said, pointing it out.

As Nancy went over to the phone, Sean checked out the tool rack. Then he opened a drawer and froze.

"Hey," he muttered, "she's been messing with my stuff. What— It's gone! She must've taken it!" His knees gave way and he collapsed into a chair, his face pasty white.

"What's gone?" Ned asked. "What's happened?"

"My gun," Sean whispered. "I keep it in here and it's gone. It's got to be Tina—"

"You have a *gun?*" Nancy's heart was racing.

"It's a dangerous neighborhood," Sean protested. "I have to protect myself, don't I?"

"Do you have a permit?" Nancy asked. Sean scowled and said nothing.

"That figures," Nancy said, reaching for the phone. But there was no dial tone. The phone was dead.

She pulled on the cord to the jack. It had been torn loose and the plug was gone.

"Tina didn't want you calling anyone for a while," she said, looking at Sean. "Let's get moving!" When Sean didn't move, Nancy said, "You, too."

"Me?" Sean asked. "You want me to go looking for Tina, when she's running wild with a gun? Uh-uh, no way!"

"You think you're in trouble now?" Nancy said. "When Tina shoots someone with your unregistered weapon, you'll see what real trouble can be. This is your chance to undo the damage you've helped to cause. Let's go!"

Sean pouted but allowed himself to be propelled by Ned out the door and to Evan's car. He slouched in the back seat while Ned and Nancy got into the front.

"Where to—Top Flight?" Ned asked.

"As fast as you can make it," Nancy said. "If a police car wants to pull us over for speeding, we can bring them along for reinforcement." She turned to Sean, who was sitting sullenly behind her. "Better fasten that seat belt. It may be a wild ride."

Evan's car had a powerful engine and was

designed to handle well. Ned stomped on the gas pedal, and they roared off, making a tight right turn and zooming up a hill.

At the top of the hill a car swung out of a parking place without signaling. Ned swerved to the left, missing the other car's fender by inches.

"Some drivers are a real menace," Ned said.

The rest of the ride was tense and silent until Ned said, "Here we are," as he nosed the car into a parking place.

"Let's hope we beat Tina," Nancy said, as they ran inside, "or that Marty is out somewhere."

The blond receptionist looked up, startled, as the threesome burst into the Top Flight office.

"Is Marty in?" Nancy asked.

"Yes, but he's— Hey, wait!" the woman protested.

Ned, Sean, and Nancy charged into Marty's office. The agent was talking on the phone.

"What is this?" he demanded, looking annoyed. "Something's come up, I'll call you back," he said into the phone, then hung up.

Marty scowled at Nancy. "What do you think you're doing, busting in like this?" he demanded. "Who's *this* guy?"

The harried receptionist appeared behind the three intruders. "I'm sorry, Mr. Prince," she said. "They ran right by before I knew what was happening."

"We have to talk, Marty," Ned said. "Right now. It's about Tina."

The agent smiled at the receptionist. "It's all right, Claire. I'll handle this."

"Can I go to lunch?" Claire asked.

"Sure," Marty said, waving her off. Then he spread out his hands in a puzzled gesture. "What about Tina?" he said. "Has she been telling wild stories? You shouldn't believe what she says about me. She's a sick girl."

"You're right about that," Nancy snapped. "Tina *is* disturbed. This is Sean McKearn, who used to be her boyfriend."

"What does this have to do with me?" Marty tried to look like a picture of injured innocence. "As I said before, Tina bugged me to take her as a client, and I turned her down. She pleaded and even threatened, and all I ever told her was no. What's so terrible about that?" he asked.

"We know you had a pipeline into JZA," Nancy said, sitting down. Ned and Sean sat on the couch beside her chair. "You always knew what was going on at JZA as soon as it happened. When Ned signed his contract and got the King Kola commercial, you knew immediately. Tina is the only one who could have told you, other than Jane herself and Evan Chandler. You promised Tina work if she kept you informed, and then you cut her loose."

"Prove it," Marty said with a smug grin.

"That's not why we're here," Ned said. "Believe it or not, we've come to help you."

Marty snorted. "Help me? By making wild accusations? Help like that I can do without."

"We thought you'd want to know that Tina has a gun," Nancy said. "Of course, if she has no reason to want you hurt, then never mind."

Marty's tan face suddenly paled, and he swallowed hard. "Gun?" he said. "Is this some kind of gag? Because it isn't funny."

"No gag, Marty," Nancy said. "Tina wants revenge. Did you know she was doing other things in an effort to put you in her debt? Like sending actors unsigned notes, threatening them if they didn't sign at Top Flight?"

"What?" Marty gasped.

"And someone was making late-night phone calls, harassing people," Ned said. "Was that Tina, or you? And did you know about the Top Flight business card that was found in Ursula Biemann's purse, right beside her body?"

Marty could only gape, speechless.

Ned leaned forward. "Remember the hot-air balloon sequence I was shooting yesterday? Someone tampered with the balloon and I almost got killed, along with two other people. We found a note saying that the company should've used Top Flight talent. It was on your personal stationery."

Marty looked from Nancy to Ned and back, chewing nervously on his lower lip. "I didn't know. I had nothing to do with that stuff. It's

145

Tina. She's gone bananas," he said, his voice hoarse. "Totally flipped out, I'm telling you."

"I'm not crazy, Marty," a voice said from behind Nancy's chair.

Nancy swung around and found Tina standing in the doorway, glaring at the agent. In her right hand she held a pistol, its barrel pointed steadily at Marty's chest. Her blue eyes glittered unnaturally.

"I am not crazy," she repeated. "But I *am* angry." Her eyes skimmed the room. "Oh, good, Sean's here, too. How convenient. Everyone stay right where you are."

Tina smiled wickedly. "It's payback time."

Chapter

Seventeen

"TINA, TAKE IT EASY," Marty croaked, staring at the gun. "Let's talk, okay?"

"You're a good talker," Tina said, shutting the door behind her. "But you're bad at keeping your word. 'Just help me out and you'll get lots of work,' you said. So I told you what was happening at JZA. And I did more. One day when you were away from your desk, I took some of your notepaper. I wrote actors little notes to get them to sign with you, and I made phone calls, too. I was on your team, Marty, and you dumped me."

"Tina," Nancy said, speaking gently, "I know you've been treated badly, but—"

"Shut up!" Tina snapped. "You told me to tell the police what I know. If I'd done that, I'd be sitting in jail right now. You're not my friend."

"Be reasonable," Marty said, giving Tina a

shaky smile that didn't reach his eyes. "Claire will have called the police by now and—"

"Wrong, Marty," Tina said, circling to his side with the gun trained on him. "I saw her leave before I came in."

"You're not a killer by nature," Nancy said, trying to speak calmly and quietly.

"No? Tell that to Ursula. I'm a killer now. And these two"—she waved the gun at Marty and Sean—"made me what I am. They're going to pay the price."

Nancy heard a strange whimpering sound. She saw that Sean was hunched forward with his arms around his knees. He was crying.

Tina looked at Ned. "I really didn't mean for anyone to be hurt in that balloon, though. I just wanted to put Marty on the spot. Really."

"Did you mean to kill Ursula?" Nancy asked. She wanted to keep Tina talking. As long as she talked, she wasn't likely to shoot.

"It doesn't matter, now. I called her and said we had to talk, that I would pick her up that night." Tina grinned at Nancy. "She actually thought we were friends. Can you believe that? She didn't have a clue." Tina chuckled to herself. "I had taken a mallet from Sean's studio. Did you know I had your key, Sean? You should change the lock when you change girls."

Tina went on. "I wanted Ursula to stop taking things from me. She took Sean and she took all the work at JZA, and she wanted to take all the work at Top Flight. It wasn't fair. She had it all and left me nothing."

Nancy saw that Ned was poised for a chance to go for the gun. But neither Sean nor Marty looked as if they'd be of any help.

"Ursula got in my car, and I said she had to stop stealing from me," Tina continued. "But she saw the mallet and started to scream and jumped out. I got out and hit her to make her stop. I keep work gloves in my car, so I put them on—I know about fingerprints. Then I dragged her into the car. There were no witnesses. I took her where she was working the next day and left her in that alley. Wasn't I nice? I made sure she kept her last appointment, and I put Marty's card in her purse."

"And you put the mallet in Ursula's wastebasket?" Nancy asked. As long as Tina wanted to talk, Nancy would play for time.

"Right," Tina replied. "I went back up and dropped it in the trash. Then I got some letters from Marty that Ursula had shown me, wrote some notes on Top Flight paper, and left them for the police to find. Marty deserved to take the blame!"

"Sure he did." Ned spoke softly, persuasively. "When people hear what really happened, they'll understand. They'll give you help." He started out of his chair.

"No!" Tina shrieked as she swung the gun toward Ned. "Sit down. Now!"

Ned slowly sat again.

Tina stood beside Marty and placed the barrel of the gun against his head. The agent's breathing became ragged. "Marty, admit what you did was wrong. Say it!" she demanded.

"I don't know what you're talking about," Marty insisted. His face was bloodless.

"Okay. You're a liar, and you'll die a liar." Tina cocked the hammer with a click.

"Marty, tell her what she wants to hear!" Nancy shouted.

"Okay!" screamed the agent. "It was wrong! I strung you along! Now put away the gun!"

Tina shook her head. "It's too little and too late. Goodbye, Marty."

Nancy considered a jump for Tina's gun arm, but the table was in the way, and she knew she'd never make it. She felt paralyzed, powerless.

"Wait, there's more!" Marty babbled, his eyes rolling around to catch Tina's. "I set the fire at JZA. I knew one big setback would put them over the edge. I made it look like arson so Jane wouldn't get the insurance. Okay? I'm spilling my guts. Don't shoot!" He cringed away from the gun.

Tina backed away a step and turned to the others. "All right, Sean, you first," she said. "You started it all, anyway. I was happy with you, and I haven't been happy since you dumped me."

As she raised the gun, Sean shrieked and flung

himself sideways out of his chair. Frowning, Tina turned to follow him.

"Ned! Now!" Nancy shouted, seeing Tina's attention focused wholly on Sean.

Ned launched himself into a low dive just as the pistol went off with a deafening roar. The shot hit the wall behind Sean. Ned grabbed Tina's wrist and forced the weapon upward. A second shot buried itself in the ceiling.

Tina tried to rake Ned's face with her nails, but he bent back, twisting the gun handle out of her grasp. She collapsed in a sobbing heap.

For a moment the room was silent except for the sound of Tina's sobs.

Sean slowly got to his feet. "She tried to kill me," he growled. He moved toward Tina, his face red with fury. "I ought to—"

Ned grabbed Sean's shoulder and spun him around. "You ought to sit down and keep your mouth shut," he snapped. He shoved Sean back into his chair, then turned to Nancy. "Nan, are you all right?" he asked.

She looked up at him and nodded.

Tina now lay silently, staring at the wall. Her face was slack and empty of expression.

"You can't use anything I said against me!" Marty shouted. "I said it at gunpoint—it wasn't true."

"You didn't start the fire at JZA?" Nancy asked.

"No!" Marty was gaining more self-assurance with Tina disarmed and defenseless.

"Then one thing puzzles me." Nancy fixed her eyes on Marty. "How did you know that the alarms and sprinklers at JZA didn't work?"

Marty blinked. "What?"

"The day we first talked to you, you said that Jane should sue the company that installed the alarms and sprinklers," Nancy said. "How did you know they didn't work?"

Ned stared at Nancy, then at Marty. "Hey, that's right. He did say something like that."

"I . . ." Marty hesitated for a moment. "The police—I heard it from them!"

"We'll have to ask Lieutenant Antonio and Inspector Matsuda if they mentioned it to you," Nancy said. "Because if they didn't, there's only one way you could have known that—if you set the fire yourself and made sure the alarms and sprinklers didn't work."

Marty swallowed and closed his eyes. His self-assurance was suddenly gone.

Ned sat on the arm of Nancy's chair and put his arm around her. She leaned against him. Looking at Tina's motionless body, Nancy felt drained.

"Tina?" Ned called. There was no response.

"She doesn't hear you," Nancy said quietly. "I think she's in her own world right now. Let's call the police and wrap this up. It's time to put it behind us."

* * *

"I wonder if Tina will come around." Jane Zachary's eyes were solemn as she spoke.

It was late that afternoon. Tina had been taken into custody and, according to Lieutenant Antonio, would get a psychiatric examination to determine if she was fit to stand trial. Her fingerprints had been found on the valve of the balloon, and the handwriting on the threatening letters hidden at Ursula's had been matched with Tina's. Sean was under arrest for his assault on Nancy, and Marty had been charged with arson.

Jane was in her office with Ned, Nancy, and Evan Chandler. She had gotten a full account of what had happened earlier that day.

"I told the police that I'll press charges against Sean," Nancy said. "With his prior record, I imagine he'll do time. As for Marty, the lieutenant is certain that he didn't learn about the alarms and sprinklers from the police. Marty wanted the fire to look like arson so that Jane couldn't collect the insurance money. The arson charge will probably hold up."

"Which means that he's through as an agent," Jane said with satisfaction. "His contracts will no longer be valid, and the people signed with him will be free to go elsewhere. My guess is that, with Marty out of the picture, Top Flight is through."

"How will Jane Zachary Associates do, now that Top Flight Artists is no longer a threat?" Ned asked.

"I expect that we'll eventually re-sign most of the people who left," Jane replied. "This experience has been a lesson to me. I think our position as the top agency in the city had made us a little complacent. I'm going to see to it that we don't lose our edge in the future. The next time some ambitious agent starts up, we'll keep our clients loyal, because we'll earn it."

"What about you, Ned?" Evan asked. "I forgot to tell you in all the excitement, Freddy wants to reschedule that King Kola commercial in a few days. Would the end of the week be all right?"

Ned and Nancy looked into each other's eyes for a moment before Ned spoke.

"Can I get out of it?" he asked. "I've given it some thought, and right now, all I really want to do is get in a few days of real vacation time with Nancy before I go back to school."

Nancy reached over and gave Ned's hand an affectionate squeeze.

"Don't worry about it, Ned," Jane assured him. "We'll find Freddy someone else for the job, and I'll make sure that he understands."

"Was it that business with the balloon that put you off?" Evan asked. "Because I believe they've decided to do something entirely different, and completely safe."

"It's not that," Ned said. "I feel as if I've been on some kind of crazy amusement park ride for the last few days. Maybe I've got some acting talent, I don't know. I don't much care. Right now, the only role I want to play is Ned Nickerson. And the only script I care about is real life. There's nothing quite like it."

His brown eyes shone as he smiled at Nancy. "Especially when I have the right person to share it with."

Nancy's next case:

The former home of author Dorothea Burden is now a meeting place and museum for mystery buffs. But Nancy's weekend at the estate turns out to be much more than an innocent exercise in fictional felonies. In fact, life imitates art . . . as murder makes a call on Mystery Mansion!

First, several jewel-encrusted figurines are stolen from the safe. The plot thickens even further when the author's longtime editor is found dead in her room. Strangest of all, in a case as tricky and treacherous as the mansion's secret passageways, Nancy is convinced that Dorothea Burden herself left behind the key to the killer's identity . . . in *THE PERFECT PLOT*, Case #76 in the Nancy Drew Files™.